The Dreaming Pool

Gary Greenwood

This book was first published in 1998 by
RazorBlade Press, 186 Railway St, Splott, Cardiff, CF2
2NH.

The Dreaming Pool is a work of collected fiction.
The characters and events described are imaginary and
any
resemblance to people living or dead is purely
coincedental.

Designed and typeset by
RazorBlade Press and John Phelps

Printed and bound in the U.K by Redwood Books,
Trowbridge.

British Library in Publication Data.
A catalogue record for this book is available
from the British Library

ISBN 0-9 531468-7-1

To ly
with love and thanks
for putting up with me

and

to my grandad
who showed me how to read books.

Introduction
By Simon Clark

It's Monday the 20th July, 1998. The BBC are coming to my home town of Doncaster. I've been invited to their event billed as BBC LISTENS. Britain at the tail end of the millennium has its own brand of Glasnost. Even the biggest corporations now crave approval from the smallest members of the public.

So, I go along, enjoy the buffet, drink their wine. Ask questions.

Then the team from the BBC ask us questions. "What's your favourite programme?" invites a BBC News Presenter bussed up north for the event. A teenager replies, "The X-Files?." The News Presenter asks a deceptively simple question: "Why do you like The X-Files?"

The teenager is stumped. He shakes his head, his cheeks go pink, he smiles uncomfortably, then says at last, "I don't know. I just like it." The teenager isn't stupid. But if you are put on the spot and asked just why exactly you like a certain programme, or book or song for that matter, it's difficult to utter a completely sensible reply. After all, much of the appeal might be to the heart as well as the mind.

So when I was asked to read and write an introduction to Gary Greenwood's The Dreaming Pool I said "Yes." Now the reading part was no problem. I enjoyed it enormously. But the difficult bit comes right now. Why do I like it? Is it something about the prose style? Is it something about the characters? Or is it the story?

Well, yes, it's all of those; but it isn't so easy to reach into a story and pluck out the element that grabs you and cries, "By Heaven, this is good!" What's more, I didn't know anything about Gary Greenwood; I've never read any of his earlier work, so I had nothing to fall back on. Nothing, that is, except The Dreaming Pool.

Now most writers of introductions would cheat a little here and comment that the book reminds them of a Stephen King, or a Lovecraft or a Clive Barker. But nope. Gary's not going to let me get away with that one. He's an original.

Yes, I can say this is an intelligent horror; the characters are three dimensional; they demand your attention, and yes — definitely yes — this is a punchy read with a damn good plot. But I think what really grabbed me (and what will grab you) is that Gary has written this from the heart. Instead of being 'inspired' by other writers or films he has been inspired to write this from life itself. The result is gritty and realistic; that realism punctures the under-belly of your psyche and worms its way deep into the guts of your brain.

There's no doubt about it: Gary Greenwood is a fresh, new talent. I don't know what he's doing now as I write this on the 24th July, 1998, but I have this unshakeable feeling that in a couple of years from now his life will have changed out of all recognition. He'll have either been contracted to write a string of novels or some television or film scripts. Either way, once you've read this book, keep it carefully tucked away on its shelf (in a nice dry room, away from the bright sunlight, mind!) and perhaps play extra safe and slip it into a plastic bag. Why? Because it's going to be a collector's item one day.

Now, I've had my say. So I'm stepping back for Gary Greenwood to have his...

Simon Clark
Doncaster, South Yorkshire. 1998.

"I will open my mouth in a parable: I will utter dark sayings of old"
Psalm 78, v2
King James Bible

Alphabetical thanks are due to the following who have given me the encouragement, criticism and kind words that have kept me writing through the last few years:

Kris Benkin, Simon Bestwick, Dave Bull, Simon Clark, Darren Floyd, David Green, Richard Hayward, Steve Hollister, Tim Lebbon, Max O'Hagan, Sean Quarterly, Sally Rand, Bill Rogers, Darren Wilcox and Matt Williams.

The Dreaming Pool

1: FRIDAY

"Jack? Jack? Phone."
The girl shook his shoulder again, trying to wake him while the telephone kept ringing next to her on the bedside table. "Jack?"

"Mmm, what?" he murmured, turning towards her slightly, running his hand over his face.

"The phone, Jack." she said, almost completely awake now. "It's ringing." She watched as he sat up in bed, the covers falling around his waist.

"Christ, it's half three in the morning." Jack Bradley said as he brought the alarm clock closer to his half-open eyes. He glanced over at the girl who still had her hand on his shoulder, rocking him gently and was more than a little alarmed to realise he couldn't remember her name. "All right," he said, shrugging her hand off.

"The phone, Jack," she repeated.

"Yeah, I can hear it." He leaned over her, still half-asleep and still half-drunk from the party where he'd met her (what the hell was her name?) and picked up the phone. "Yeah?"

"Jack? It . . . it's your mum." She sniffed, holding back tears.

"How did you get my phone number?"

"I phoned Matt. Jack? It's your dad. He's . . ." She started to sob, crying down the phone at him.

"What happened?" he asked stiffly. His mother didn't answer for a minute or so, just hung on the phone crying. "Mum? What happened?" he asked again, a little gentler.

"He's dead, Jack," she managed, crying all the while. "He's dead." Jack sighed and ran a hand through his hair. The girl in his bed poked him with a finger to get his attention. "What's wrong?" she whispered.

"One second, Mum," Jack said and dropped the phone on the floor. He stood up and climbed over the girl (Eve, her name was Eve) and went over to the far wall where he turned the light on, scrunching his eyes up against the sudden light. Eve quickly dove under the covers to save her own vision becoming accustomed to the brightness. Jack sat back down on the edge of the bed, picked up the phone in one hand and a pencil from the bedside table in the other.

"Mum? Give me your phone number. There's no point

in talking now. I'll phone you in the morning." He scribbled the number on the notepad as she read it out to him, dropping the pencil when he'd finished. "Okay, I'll ring you tomorrow. This morning, whatever. Yeah. Bye." With a sigh, he hung up the phone and went to turn the light off.

"What's wrong?" Eve asked.

"Nothing," he said. "Go back to sleep."

"Phone calls in the middle of the night are usually something," she said, sitting up, her back against the headboard. He glanced at her nakedness in the half-light as he clambered into bed beside her, but instead of answering he put his head on the pillow and tried to get back to sleep.

"You want a cup of tea?" Jack asked as Eve entered the kitchen.

"Please," she said, sidling up to him and pecking him on the cheek as he filled the kettle.

"There's some toast there as well if you want some," he said, nodding his head toward the table where a plate of golden buttered toast sat.

"So who was that on the phone this morning?" Eve asked, biting into a slice of toast as she put on her high heels.

"My mother, ringing to tell me my dad's dead," Jack said. He dropped a couple of tea bags into the pot.

"Seriously?" Eve asked. "Babes, I'm sorry. You okay?"

"I'm fine." Truth to tell, Jack wasn't fine at all. He'd had very little sleep thanks to Eve before the phone call and his mother's message afterwards, coupled with the fact that he was nursing one of the worst hangovers he'd had for a long time.

"So what you gonna do?" Eve asked. Jack looked over at her as he filled the teapot with boiling water: her hair was neatly done, her makeup replaced, her party dress sensible enough to be worn to work this morning with the jacket she'd brought with her. He sighed.

"Phone her up and find out what's going on."

"How come you didn't have her number?" Another slice of toast began to disappear.

"We don't talk much," Jack answered simply, bringing the tea over. As soon as he sat down opposite her, Eve stood and walked around the table, sitting on his lap and putting her arm around his shoulder. "Get off me," Jack said, pushing her from him.

"Hey, I was only trying to console you, Babes." Eve said, pouting.

"Well thanks, but I don't need consoling from you."

"Fine." She threw the half-eaten piece of toast on the table and pulled her jacket on. "I suppose I'd better get to work, then." Her tone mellowed and she smiled. "I'll come straight here from work, okay?"

"I'd rather you didn't," Jack said, sipping at his tea.
Eve looked at him, thunderclouds gathering over her head.

"So that's it? I'm a one night stand?" Jack met her gaze and watched as her lower lip began to tremble. "I thought we had something, Babes?", she said.

"We did," he said. "Sex, last night."

As he took another sip of his tea, she lashed out, hitting the cup and splashing hot liquid over his arm. "Shit!" he hissed, shifting back in his chair, toppling it over and landing almost upside down.

"Fuck you!" she screamed at him, throwing the toast on top of him for good measure, before running back upstairs. A moment later she was back, handbag in hand, and without another word she stormed out of the door.

Jack stood and made his way over to the sink, picking up a tea towel and wetting it under the tap before running it all over his stinging arm. He looked over at the chair covered in tea and toast and down at his dressing gown which hung in much the same state and began to chuckle. He carried on laughing as he tidied up himself and the kitchen only stopping when he remembered his mother's telephone call last night.

"Hello?"

"It's Jack."

"Well, yew took yewr time ringing back." Jack sighed; his sister had answered the phone. "Mum's bin worried sick up yer waiting for yew."

"Can I speak with her?" he said, rubbing at his forehead, trying to massage away the headache that was getting bigger with each word that his sister yelled down the phone at him. Jack's earlier comment about not talking much with his family had been an understatement, to say the least: it had been almost seven years since he had had any but the most cursory contact with any of his family, with the exception of his brother Matthew. The few times he had seen his mother had been when she had visited him in the shop where he had worked, visits which inevitably left him uncomfortable and embarrassed. Since leaving the shop, however, he had quite gratefully lost all contact.

"Jack?" his mother said.

"What happened, Mum?"

She sniffed loudly. Jack wondered whether she had been crying continuously since half three that morning. Probably, he guessed.

"He went up to the corner shop to get a paper a couple of days ago and didn't come back. The police found him yesterday. Oh, Jack, he . . . he . . . " She broke off, crying and sobbing.

"What happened to him?" Jack asked, but there was no reply, only the sound of his mother crying further away from the phone.

"Did yew ave to talk to er?" his sister suddenly yelled. He winced, partly at the volume, partly at her harsh Welsh accent. "She asn't stopped crying since yesterday an' yew ad to set er off again."

"Let me talk to Matt," Jack said as calmly as he could. One of the main reasons he had left home when he was seventeen was the animosity between his sister and himself, a mutual dislike which had not diminished with the passing years.

"He's not yer yet. Mum only talked to 'im this morning." Jack heard his mother say something in the background, though he couldn't make out what it was. He stood in his living room, the phone held up to his ear, wondering how his mother had obtained his phone number from Matt if she'd only talked to him this morning. But then, he realised, she'd already spoken to him this morning as well. At half past three in the bloody morning.

"Mum wants yew to come up an' see er," his sister wailed down the phone at him. From her tone of voice it was obvious that she didn't want him to visit.

"There might be a problem with that, Di," Jack said patiently, still rubbing at his forehead. "I don't know where you live." Both Jack and his family had moved several times since they had stopped speaking with each other, so each had no idea where the other lived. His sister moaned at him for a minute or so before giving him the address. He was a little startled to find that, during the intervening years, his parents and his sister had moved back to the council estate just outside Caerphilly where he had been born and had lived until he was ten.

"Tell her I'll be up this afternoon."

"Yew better be as well." were his sister's final words to him before she slammed the phone down. Jack replaced his own handset and slumped into one of the armchairs, staring at the picture above his fireplace. It was a framed, poster-sized reproduction of an illustration by Gustav Dore, of Don Quixote tipping at windmills. Both the poor knight and his mount, Rozinante, were being hurled aloft by one of the sails, while Sancho Panza stood in the background, one hand clasped to his forehead, the other in the air, lamenting the actions of his master. "What a way to start the weekend," Jack moaned.

He reached over to where he had thrown his jacket the night before and searched around in the pockets for his cigarettes. He came up with his Zippo lighter and a crumpled packet which, aside from a few flakes in the bottom, held nothing in the way of tobacco. "Fucking typical," he muttered, throwing the empty packet on the floor. He ran a hand through his hair, bringing his feet up under him and trying to curl up in the chair, wondering what else could go wrong.

The drive up to the council estate where Jack's family lived took a little over an hour. Passing through the small towns on the way, Jack found his thoughts turning to his childhood, to memories of his youth, things he hadn't thought about for many a year. His family had moved from the estate to Newport when he was ten; his father had been working in the larger town at the time and, with Jack's grandmother coming to live with them, they needed a bigger house. His overriding memory of the move was not of large vans and possessions bundled into boxes, but rather of the first night he had spent in the new house...

By the time everything was brought down to Newport, it was evening, in the middle of December. With great fanfare, Jack's mother flipped a light switch in the main living room and discovered that the previous occupants had taken everything they owned, including the light bulbs. Jack sat in a corner, on perhaps the only chair not to be piled high with boxes and black bags, and listened as the first argument of the new house began.

"I thought you'd checked the lights?" his mother asked his father in the gloom.

"I did," he offered weakly. "They were on last night when I got the keys."

"Well, where the hell are they now?" she asked sharply. It had been a long day of moving things from one place to another and nerves and tempers were frayed. "Don't pick on Dad," Diane pitched in. Jack's sister was sixteen at the time, and over the years had acquired the habit of not so much sticking up for her father as simply being against her mother in any argument.

The situation wasn't helped by Jack's grandmother, his father's mum. "Stay out of this Di." she said.

Sides had been drawn, and as his father and sister launched an attack against his mother and gran, Jack sat almost forgotten in the dark corner, watching and listening as his family once again went forth to do battle.

Jack's brother Matt turned up at this point, having been sent to a nearby chip shop to buy them all supper. "Who ordered what?" he asked as he closed the door behind him. Standing in the hall, holding two plastic carriers full of fish and chips and God knew what else, he looked at the conflict before him and walked straight past the living room door and into the kitchen, tripping over something in the dark and cursing loudly. At fourteen, Matt had played mediator in many such arguments, even before the arrival of his gran, but tonight he was obviously not interested.

Jack, alone in the corner, watched the whole scene played out like some shadow theatre production, the street lamp outside the front window back lighting the combatants as their arms waved and heads shook. What seemed like hours later but was probably only twenty minutes, his mother stormed out of the room and up the stairs, sobbing loudly. It was only a cease fire. Instantly Diane rounded on her gran. "Look what yew've done now!" she yelled, forcing Jack's father to ease back from the front and try to calm things down between his daughter and his mother.

Perhaps an hour later, amidst a sullen, oppressive atmosphere, the whole family sat around a candle lit table eating the fresh fish and chips that Matt had again been sent out to buy, no one speaking much, his mother's eyes red and puffy from her tears. Jack looked around at each of them and for the first time in his life found himself wondering about the future.

Things never really improved after that first night. The arguments continued, the screaming and shouting never seeming to stop, and Jack found himself more and more alone. When his gran moved out, back to her other children in London, things seemed to get better for a while, but eventually Matt lost his neutrality and was drawn in to defend his mother against Diane and their father.

There was no escape for Jack even in school. Especially in school. Ridiculed by the other kids because of his strong Welsh valley's accent, he became the scapegoat and butt of all jokes in his class. His work, which had been average in his Caerphilly school, began to suffer; he had no urge to complete any of it in class and there was no encouragement at home. More and more, he was left on his own. "Oh, poor old me," he said aloud in his car, dragging his mind back from its reverie. His youth, particularly his school years, was not something he wanted to think about. He switched on the radio and hummed along to anything he knew as he drove back to the council estate to which his family had returned.

He managed to find the house without too much trouble; his parents and his sister had moved into a house on the same street where he had lived as a child. He looked at the scrap of paper on which he had jotted down their address and, after parking the car, walked up the street checking the house numbers.

Number 15 looked just like all the rest with its patch of ruined scrubland for a front garden, barely more than five feet long and strewn with toys belonging the teeming swarms of children who had been bred on the estate and who hung around it like herds of slack-jawed cattle.The front of the house held nothing more than a door and a window on the ground floor, and two windows above, all of them surrounded by peeling paint and the wonderful invention that was pebble-dash. A squat shed took up most of the garden to the other side of the front door, or maybe they'd had it converted into a coal bunker -- his mother had always been infatuated with the romantic notion of a real coal fire.

Sighing, Jack lit up a cigarette, opened the small gate and walked up the path.

"Yew were supposed to be yer ages ago," his sister said as she opened the door. Jack looked at his watch.

"It's the afternoon, exactly when I said I'd be here."

"Don't get funny with me," Diane said as Jack pushed past her ample bulk, the consequence of TV dinners and microwave meals for one, which, according to Matt, were the staples of her diet. "An' there's no smoking in the ouse," she said, following him.

"Where's Mum?" he asked, deliberately dragging on his cigarette. The past seven years or so hadn't been good to his sister, he noted (admittedly with some spiteful glee). Not only had she put on weight but her complexion was shot, her chin, nose and forehead dotted with blackheads and acne despite her thirty -six years, and her hair, which had once been long, was now cropped short, her pale scalp almost showing through in places.

"She's upstairs a minute. I'll get er." As Diane left the room and stomped heavily up to fetch his mother, Jack looked around for an ashtray. Had he been searching for a lifetime's supply of bric-a-brac and tacky china figurines he would have had no problem. Having no luck, he went over to the real coal fire that he had predicted and, picking up a mug from the mantelpiece which contained day-old coffee at the bottom, tapped his cigarette in that.

"You must be Jack, the prodigal son."

He looked over at the doorway, surprised to see a young woman standing there, wearing a charcoal grey business suit, her dark hair piled neatly on top of her head, two ringlets dropping down on either side of her small face. She smiled as she looked him up and down, taking in his faded jeans and old denim jacket.

"I must be," he said. "And you are?"

She stepped forward, offering him her hand. "I'm Rachel Lewis. I work for the crematorium."

"I didn't know they did house calls now. Are we going to burn my dad on the fire?" She smiled, a small network of lines creasing around her eyes. "Sorry. My mother is a friend of your mum's. She asked me to pop round and have a chat. I'm not really here in any professional capacity. In fact, I was just about to leave."

"What? And miss the return of the black sheep to the fold?"

"Jack?" his sister yelled from the top of the stairs. "Come up yer."

Rachel looked up at the ceiling for a second "I think I can live without that," she said, smiling back at Jack. He watched her head for the front door.

"See you at the funeral," he said. She waved without looking back.

"Jack!" Diane yelled again. He ditched his cigarette in the cup, replaced the cup on the mantelpiece and headed upstairs.

A half-hour later Jack sat on the small fence outside the house, one hand in the pocket of his denim jacket, the other holding a cigarette, watching his brother's large and impressive car pull up in the space beside his own smaller vehicle.
Matt climbed out and locked the door, the indicators blinking in time with the beeps of the car alarm. It had been almost six months since they'd last seen each other and, although Jack had let his hair grow longer since he'd finished his job and was wearing an ear ring again, he was glad to see his older brother hadn't changed. Matt was the same as ever, big and hulking in his suit and tie, his large black overcoat barely covering his frame. Jack could easily picture Matt with his square face and round glasses below a black crew cut, as a Mafia hitman.

"Hello, Jack," his brother said as he approached, sticking his hand out. They shook, Jack smiling at his formality. "How come you're out here?"

"Di was getting on my nerves about me smoking, so I thought I'd get a bit of peace and quiet."

"Have you spoken to Mum yet?"

"Yeah, though I don't know if you'd call it talking. I just kind of sat on the bed while she cried. Hardly the most stimulating of conversations."

"Can you blame her?" Matt asked. He too had lost his

Welsh accent when he was in school, but whereas Jack had been bullied out of his, Matt had dropped his through choice. Jack shrugged in answer to Matt's question, dragging on his smoke.

"Do you know if the police have released Dad's body yet?" Matt asked.

"The police? What have they got it for?"

Matt stared at him, frowning. "You don't know?" Jack shrugged again. "I thought Diane would have at least told you."

"Told me what?"

Matt sat down on the fence beside him, tucking his overcoat up underneath him. "Dad's body was found in the woods up behind the estate by the police, who were searching for a drugs stash apparently." Matt sighed and looked at his brother. "They found him at the Dreaming Pool."

"The Dreaming Pool?" Jack said.

"Yeah. You remember the place?"

"Vaguely." Jack looked over at Matt. "How did he die?"

"Someone or something had literally . . . ripped his head off his shoulders. The police found claw marks around the neck and chest from something, though whether that was dogs . . . rooting around after he'd been killed, they don't know yet."

"Jesus." Jack ditched his cigarette in the drain at the edge of the pavement. "Does Mum know all this?"

Matt shook his head. "No. I managed to have a chat with the detective inspector in charge to see if we could save telling her for a while; maybe we'll never need to."

"Jesus," Jack whispered again, reaching for another cigarette. "I thought he'd died from something to do with his heart, you know?"

Matt nodded. "Just like you will if you keep smoking that much." He sighed and stood. "I'm going to go and see Mum. You coming in?"

"Yeah, in a minute. I'll just finish this."

Matt opened the gate and walked up to the door. A moment later Jack heard it open, then close. He sat smoking in silence for a few minutes, trying not to picture his father lying cold and grey on some sparse patch of ground in this God forsaken place, his head a few feet away, staring up at the unfeeling sky.

"You okay, Jack?"

He turned to see Rachel Lewis, the young woman from the crematorium, looking at him.

"Thought you'd gone," he said with a smile.

"Like I said, my mum's a friend of your mum's. She only lives a couple of doors up so I popped in to say hi." She looked at him closely. "You okay?" she asked again.

"Yeah, I suppose so. Been better, you know?"

She stepped over to the fence and sat down next to him, tucking her skirt underneath in much the same way as Matt had done with his coat.

"Sorry about your dad," she said quietly. "I know it must be a lame thing to say, but . . . " She trailed off.

"It's not so bad. Me and the family haven't really been talking over the last few years. We had some big feud and that was it, years of silence."

"Do you mind my asking what it was about?"

Jack flicked his half-smoked cigarette away, watching it spin through the air like a poorly made firework.

"Ah, it was my fault really, I'm so fucking stubborn. We had words and lost contact with each other. After a while my mother used to visit me in this shop where I used to work and she'd try and get me to come up and see them but . . . I don't know, I just couldn't be arsed, really." He sighed and straightened up, then looked over at her. "Listen, is there somewhere I can get some food round here? I'm starving."

"There's a good cafe down in Caerphilly. They do okay meals."

Jack smiled at her and stuffed both hands into his denim jacket. "Fancy a bite to eat?"

"What about your family?" Rachel asked.

"They can get their own," he said with a grin. "Coming?" He stood up. Rachel looked up at him for a second, checked her watch, then joined him.

"Okay," she said.

"So," Rachel said before tucking in to her meal. "tell me about your family."

Jack shrugged and sprinkled first salt, then pepper on to his plate of beans, two eggs, bacon and sausages, passing them over to Rachel when he was done. He smiled as she shook them both on to her dinner, the same meal he had ordered. He was happy to find that there were normal women on the earth after all. The last few girls he had gone out with had all been vegetarians or on a diet or both, and he had become heartily sick of going to restaurants and ordering salad with low fat salad cream and extra celery for them. It was refreshing to find a girl who enjoyed cholesterol as much as he did.

"My family?" he said as the waitress brought their mugs of tea over. "What's to say? I haven't had any contact with them for about seven years."

"Okay, what about you?"

"Well, I was born and bred on the estate, lived there till I was ten."

"You don't sound Welsh." Rachel said.

"No, I suppose not. Both my parents are actually English. They moved to Caerphilly just before my sister was born, then they had my brother, then me. We moved to Newport when I was ten and the kids in the school I went to -- " said Jack shifting easily into the Welsh accent he had tried so hard to lose when he was ten " -- they took the piss outta me, like, so I ad to lose my accent, see." They smiled at each other for a second. "I left home when I was seventeen, my family moved back to Caerphilly, we had that feud I mentioned and we stopped talking. The only one I speak to now is my brother, Matt."

"What's he like?"

Jack sipped at his tea and frowned slightly. "Matt's a strange one. We've always gotten on, but we've never been really close. He lives in Cardiff now."

"Doing what?"

Jack chuckled. "Do you know, I have no idea what my brother actually does for a living? All I know is that he works for some big family firm." He stared out the window for a moment, watching the tired and listless people of Caerphilly wander past through the grey streets, with their heads down, looking only at the pavement. He looked back at Rachel. "I wouldn't be surprised if Matt has been involved in violence at some point."

It was Rachel's turn to frown. "Why do you say that?"

"Gut feeling?" Jack offered with a shrug, returning to his dinner. "Matt always gives me the impression of being a bit of a hard man, you know, someone who can take care of himself. I mean, he's a big bugger anyway, but he's got that . . . that aura about him, I suppose. I wouldn't want to meet him in a dark alley, I can tell you."

"What about your sister?" With a contented sigh, Rachel sat back in her chair and pushed her empty plate away from her. Jack laughed at her question.

"Diane's the reason I left home. It was either that or suffer a very long stretch in prison for killing her, which I probably would have done." He shook his head ruefully. "The arguments we had were ridiculous. She still doesn't like me. God knows how Mum's put up living with her for so long." Jack pushed away his own plate and picked up his tea, elbows on the table, and stared over the mug at Rachel. "Why all the questions?"

She shrugged and smiled. "Curiosity. I don't know your family that well; I haven't even met your brother, but I've met your mother and sister a couple of times when they've visited my mother and . . . I'm just surprised at how different you are."

"That's putting it lightly." Jack lit up a cigarette, offering one to Rachel who shook her head. As he flicked his Zippo open he asked, "What about you? Your family, what do you do, stuff like that."

"Not very interesting -- "

"You finished with these, luv?" the waitress asked suddenly, appearing at the side of the table. She took the plates without waiting for an answer. Jack watched as she crammed her large frame through the gap in the counter that presumably led to the kitchen at the back.

"Ah, the wonders of Welsh girls," he said with a smile.

"Hey, watch it. You're not the only one who's lived round here all their lives," Rachel said.

"You don't sound Welsh."

"Neither do you, remember?" She glanced at her watch. "Shit, I've got to get back to work. Can you drop me off at your parents' place? I left my car there."

The drive back up to the council estate was made in silence. Almost before Jack's car had stopped, Rachel was out the door and heading towards her own.

"Hey, Rachel?" Jack called as he stepped out of the driver's door. She looked back as she unlocked her car. "Listen, do you fancy . . ." was as far as he got before she said, "I'd love to. I'll give you a ring." Jack watched as she climbed in and drove off, waving to him as she went. Locking up his own car, he put another cigarette into his mouth, grinned as he lit it and walked up the path to his mother's house.

"Where the bloody ell ave you bin?" Diane shouted at him before he even got to the door. "Mum's bin askin' for you."

Jack deliberately blew smoke into his sister's face and said in his Welsh accent, "'As she? Oh, there's terrible, innit?" Stepping past her into the house, he ignored her cries about smoking inside.

"You're kidding, aren't you?" his mate Gareth asked him later that evening. He and Jack sat in their local pub in Newport, drinking their beers, tapping their feet to the music and watching the world stumble by. Jack smiled and blew smoke up to the ceiling where large fans circled lazily, pushing the grey air around the noisy room.

"Nope."

"You picked up some girl who's probably going to be burying your father next week?" "

"Cremating."

"Burying, cremating, whatever." Gareth shook his head and took one of Jack's cigarettes, lighting it with his own plastic lighter. "You gotta admit, mate, that's a bit . . . ghoulish, isn't it?"

"Not really," Jack shrugged. "We just got talking, went for a bite to eat - "

"You took her out?"

"Well, if you count going to a greasy spoon as taking somebody out, then yeah, I suppose so. Thing is, I didn't even ask if she wanted to do anything. She just . . . I don't know, she just threw me an answer to a question I hadn't even asked, if you see what I mean."

"Not really," Gareth said. He cradled his glass in both hands as if trying to warm the contents and looked around. The pub, just on the outskirts of the town centre, catered mostly for students, but on a Friday night such as this, there was also a large number of trendier types, men and women who would probably have been called yuppies a few years ago. They were slumming it getting drunk enough before going on to the night-clubs in town.

"So when is the funeral?" Gareth asked, turning back to Jack.

"Don't know. It all depends on when the police release my dad's body."

"The police? Why are they involved?"

Jack told him briefly about the condition in which his father's corpse had been discovered.

"He had his head cut off?" asked Gareth.

"Not cut off, torn off. Matt had a word with the copper in charge or something and found that out."

"Jesus. I'm sorry, man."

"Ah, no real worries. I haven't been close to my family for years, mate, you know that." Jack crushed his cigarette out in the ashtray and looked around the pub himself. Another friend of theirs had arranged to meet them here but she hadn't turned up yet.

"But even still, Jack. I mean, it's your dad, isn't it?"

Jack grinned as he drained the last of his beer. "So they say, Gar," he said, "but you know I've always claimed I was adopted."

"Yeah, right," Gareth said with a grin. "Another one?" he asked, pointing at Jack's glass. Jack handed it to him and slumped down in his seat as his friend went to the bar.

He found himself wondering about his reaction to the news of his father's death; was it some sort of show of bravado, a way of covering up the real hurt and pain he must be feeling deep inside himself ? He was a little surprised to realise that it wasn't. Jack hadn't had any real contact with his father for years , and finding out he was dead was only slightly more distressing than finding the chip shop closed when he was hungry. And what about Rachel Lewis, the crematorium worker? Gareth was right there, Jack supposed; chatting somebody up when you're visiting your grieving family did sound a little ghoulish. He hadn't meant to do it, he knew that, but at the same time he hadn't run away from it either.

"Here you go, mate." Gareth said, returning with two full pints of bitter.

"Cheers, Gar."

"So what happened with you and that Eve girl at the party last night?" Gareth asked with a leer.

Jack laughed and lit up another cigarette.

"Mind your own fucking business, mate," he said.

"Oh, come on. You know as well as I do she couldn't keep her eyes off you as soon as you walked into the place. You shag her?" he asked with a wicked glint in his eye.

"We went back to my place, spent the night together and then this morning, after I'd found out about my dad, she just turned into Claire Raynor."

"How do you mean?"

Jack sighed, remembering the events of that morning. "She just came over all serious, you know? Acted as if we'd been going out for about a year or something, calling me Babes, wanting to come back and comfort me and stuff. Last thing I wanted, you know?"

"So she's still single then?"

Jack looked over at Gareth. Even though he was twenty-eight, he still dressed as Jack and all his other friends had when they were sixteen and into heavy metal - a scruffy leather jacket with a denim jacket, the arms ripped off, worn over it, covered with badges and patches of bands that had faded away much as the embroidered cotton had done. Jack's friend not only had the dress sense of a teenager, he still had the complexion, his face riddled with bright red acne and the scars of spots gone by; Whether it was some sort of hormonal imbalance or more to do with Gareth's eating habits Jack didn't know. Gareth's hair wasn't in much better condition either: long, straight and always lank and lifeless. "Yeah, she's still single." Jack said with an indulgent smile. How Gareth had managed to get an invite to the previous night's party still baffled Jack. He must have known about three people there and, with the exception of Jack, none of them had wanted to talk with him.

"How long have we known each other, mate?" Jack asked.

Gareth frowned, more baffled at the question than wondering about the answer. "Since we were ten or eleven, I suppose. Why's that?"

"Oh, no reason," Jack replied with a smirk. During all that time, he had known Gareth to go out with only one girl, a lovely, kind-hearted girl named Tara who, for some reason unknown to Jack and his other friends, had taken a real shine to Gareth when he was 19. Sadly, the day after the pair had gone out on their first date, Tara had been run over by a bus. Try as he might, Jack could never stop himself laughing at the irony of it, despite the situation's gruesome overtones.

"I gotta have a piss," Jack said, standing up and making his way through the crowded bar to the toilets on the other side of the pub. Pushing open the door, he found the spaces at the trough full so he headed to one of the two cubicles, nudging the door closed behind him but not bothering to lock it. Standing there and peeing into the bowl, Jack wondered whether Gareth would ask Eve out. Probably not, he thought. Gareth had been terrified of girlfriends and relationships ever since poor Tara.

Someone knocked on the cubicle door. "Give us a minute, mate," Jack called over his shoulder. Suddenly the door swung inwards, hitting him in the back, making him stumble towards the toilet and barking his shins on the bowl. "What the fuck --" was all he managed before someone pushed him face first into the rear wall, holding him there with what felt like a very big hand. Jack heard the door being locked behind him. Oh shit, I'm gonna get fucked, was all he could think. He struggled against the man's hand, but with his legs on either side of the bowl and his hands still in front of him holding his dick there wasn't much he could do.

The man pulled him back, then slammed him forward again, this time grabbing his arms and pinning them behind his back. Stars and rockets went off in Jack's head and he felt his eyes fill up with water. He wondered whether his nose was broken and tasted blood in his mouth.

"Listen to me, Bradley." The man's voice was quiet, insistent. "Next week, you're going to bury your father."

"Cremate," Jack muttered. He was pulled back and slammed into the wall again.

"Don't fucking cheek me, Bradley. Next week you'll cremate your father and then you will go about your life. Forget your father. Forget the Dreaming Pool. Forget the whole damn thing. You understand me?"

"Yeah, I speak English," Jack said before he could stop himself. His face met the wall again and this time he was sure he'd heard his nose break. "Yeah, I understand," he said.

The next instant the door was unlocked and his assailant was gone. Jack stood for a minute, leaning against the wall, still with his legs around the toilet and his jeans hanging around his legs.

He groaned and pushed himself upright. "Fuck, that hurt," he said, gently rubbing his nose.

"Fucking shirt lifter."

Jack turned to see some guy in a suit and tie looking at him, his face full of disgust and outrage, with the emphasis on rage. Looking down at his dishevelled state and at his surroundings, Jack thought it didn't take a genius to work out what Mr Executive was thinking. With as much dignity as he could muster, Jack tucked himself in and walked out of the cubicle, glancing at his bruised and bloodied face in the mirror as he left.

"What the fuck happened to you?" Gareth cried as Jack returned to the table.

"Let's go and I'll tell you all about it," he said, lifting up his jacket and heading for the door while ignoring the looks from the other drinkers.

Gareth stood with a can of bitter in the hallway of Jack's house while Jack himself stood in the downstairs toilet, a clump of damp toilet roll held to his nose. He carefully dabbed at it to clear away the dried blood, wincing every time the cool tissue touched his skin.

"So he just had a go at you in the bogs?" Gareth asked.

"Yeah," Jack replied. "Told me to forget about my dad as well."

"What's he got to do with your dad?"

"How the fuck would I know?" Jack called, turning to look at his friend. "I'm in there having a piss and some bastard shoves me up against the cubicle wall." He looked back at the mirror and inspected his nose. "I thought I was going to get fucking raped, I tell you."

Gareth sniggered. Jack looked at him again. "It wasn't fucking funny, mate. Jesus." He tossed the blood stained paper down the toilet, pulled some more off the roll and gently dried his already swollen nose.

"Is it broken?" Gareth asked, handing Jack a can of beer as he came out.

"I don't think so. Hurts like fuck, though." The pair went

through into Jack's living room and slumped into the chairs. An expensive hi-fi sat in one corner, vinyl albums and CDs racked up beneath it with a small collection of tapes sitting to one side. In the opposite corner, in their own wooden cabinet, lived Jack's TV and video, again with his tapes arranged beneath them. Along every wall, with the exception of the one where the Gustav Doré, print hung, ran shelves, stuffed with books.

"Something else he said which was a bit strange." Gareth looked at Jack. "He told me to forget about the Dreaming Pool as well as my dad."

"What's that?" Gareth went over to the hi-fi and began to look through Jack's CDs.

"Put something mellow on. Nothing heavy," Jack said, carefully touching his nose. A moment later *Solitude Standing* by Suzanne Vega started up.

"I never thought I'd be putting something like this on," Gareth moaned, going back to his chair. Jack smiled. "So?" Gareth prompted him.

"Years ago, I lived on a council estate just outside Caerphilly. There was the main town," Jack said leaning forward as he spoke and drawing out the directions with his finger on the coffee table, "and a road which goes out towards Abertridwr. You go past one estate, Penyrheol, then up a hill to the estate where my parents live. That road in turn meets up with another road which runs round the entire bunch of houses, kind of like a ring road, encircling the whole thing. Then there are the avenues and culs -de -sacs actually leading into the estate itself. On the side of the estate opposite where the road from town meets the ring road, there's a really dense wooded area that stretches up to the top of the hill that the estate's built on. In those woods is the Dreaming Pool.

"There was a rumour or a legend or whatever going round the estate, when I was about six or seven, that nobody could find the Pool unless they'd already dreamed of it and that those who tried without having dreamed about the place first would always end up lost in the woods. Probably because of those stories I dreamed about a pool in the woods when I was seven, I think, and not long after I told my brother Matt about it. One Saturday, when my parents and my sister were off doing something, he took me on a walk into the woods, telling me to bring my shorts and a towel.

"I followed Matt on that sunny afternoon into the woods at the top of the estate . It seemed like we walked for miles, though it probably wasn't that far, until we reached a small area of level ground, like a miniature plateau on the hill. In the centre of that was the Dreaming Pool. As I remember, it was huge, about ten feet wide and twenty feet long, and the water in it was weird. There were already a few kids there, maybe a dozen or so, but they hardly gave me and Matt a second glance. So, following Matt's lead, I got undressed and put my shorts on, dumping my clothes over to one side near everyone else's. One of the things I remember most about that place was watching Samantha Bond climbing out of the Pool in her bikini. She must have been only about twelve or thirteen, but I just remember staring at her, fascinated by her body, the first girl I ever saw in a bikini." Jack smiled and sipped at his beer.

"Anyhow, Matt just climbed in and started splashing around, doing the usual kid -in -a -pool type of stuff, you know? But I hung back, staring at the water. It wasn't like normal water; there seemed to be something in in, some sort of crystals which reflected the sunlight, making the whole Pool look as if it had stars in it. The bottom of the Pool was odd as well, all knobbly like coral but the colours of different metals like gold and copper. It scared me a bit, I must admit, but after Matt turned round and called for me to jump in, I figured what the hell and climbed in."

"What happened?" Gareth asked.

"Nothing much.I climbed in and splashed around with my brother and the other kids that were there and had a good laugh. After a while, though, I went over to one corner of the Pool, away from most of the other kids just to catch my breath, like." Jack sipped again at his beer and lit up a cigarette, staring at the flame of his Zippo for a minute before clicking it shut.

"I was just standing there in the corner, watching the other kids having a good time, feeling happy with the world, minding my own business." He looked over at his friend. "Something brushed past my legs. Something warm. I looked down, but all I could see were the reflections in the strange water. I thought I must have imagined it, then something wrapped itself around my legs and pulled.

"I went under, completely covered. Water went up my nose and in my mouth. I couldn't feel the floor or the sides of the Pool. I couldn't see anything and my ears were full of water. I was suspended, cut off from everything. Everything except the feeling of whatever it was that held my legs and was still pulling me, deeper and deeper. I thrashed about, trying to get free or grab hold of the edge of the Pool, but I couldn't find anything. All there was, was just this thing pulling me down further into the water, which became colder and colder." He sipped at his can again.

"Then I broke free. Or it let me go. One second I was in what I'd imagined to be fifteen, twenty feet of water, the next I'm standing on the Pool's bottom, then I'm breaking through the surface of the water, coughing and retching. I don't remember much of what happened next, but my brother told me I went nuts, started screaming and yelling, crawling out of the pool and jabbering on about sea monsters and things."

Jack smiled at his friend who sat, listening avidly. "What then?" Gareth asked.

Jack shrugged. "Not much. At least, not much to do with me. I'd had such a scare I never went there again. Nobody else did after some young boy was killed up there."

"A kid was killed?"

"Yeah. I don't remember much, but apparently some kid from the estate was found by the Pool towards the end of that summer. He'd been ... 'interfered with' was the phrase, but I didn't know what that meant until I grew up a bit. After that, no one went up to the Dreaming Pool as far as I know, and I'd forgotten all about it until the last day or two." He chuckled. "Tell you one thing, though: when a bunch of us kids went to see Star Wars the following year, I practically shit myself during that scene in the garbage disposal unit."

Gareth laughed and the conversation turned to other films and music, the pair chatting together until Jack called a halt to the evening and politely kicked his friend out of his house.

"Hi Jack," Jack said from the urinal as he walked in. He nodded to himself and went into one of the cubicles, closing the door behind him. Jack from the urinal went into the other

toilet and, lowering the seat, stood on it and looked over into the first where he saw himself taking a leak. Then there was a man behind Jack, in the first cubicle, though the watcher couldn't see his face. Instead of pushing Jack up against the wall, the man took a knife and pulled Jack's head back, cutting it off in one sweep and dropping it in the toilet bowl.

The Jack who was watching yelled out and rushed from his toilet into the other cubicle. The man was gone, as was the other Jack's body, but his head still floated in the water. The door behind Jack closed and locked and he kicked at it as the water in the bowl began to rise, his own head bobbing against the rim. "Don't forget to forget the Dreaming Pool," his disembodied head whispered as the cubicle began to fill with water. "Don't forget to forget the Dreaming Pool." The water was around his groin .

"Ah, fucking hell," Jack said, reaching down to his crotch which was warm and wet. He flung the covers back and climbed out of the sodden mess of sheets and quilt, wiping ineffectually at his thighs, shivering as the cold air twisted around his legs like a cat that had just been let in.

Cursing under his breath all the time, Jack stripped the bed, balling up the sheets and the quilt into one pile and stuffing it into a corner near the washing basket . Then he stumbling out into the hall, heading for the bathroom in some confusion. The last time he had wet the bed had been when he was a child, still living in Caerphilly.

Jack winced as he pulled the light cord in the bathroom, his eyes screwing up against the harsh intrusion of brightness. Then he reached into the shower and turned it on, holding his hand under the spray until it warmed up enough to climb in.

Jack washed himself thoroughly, disliking the idea of wetting the bed more than the actual fact of it, unsure just why he should have done it. But then, he thought, not everybody has their father killed and then gets beaten up in a pub because of it, all in one day. He rinsed himself off, turned off the shower and stepped out, wrapping one towel from the radiator around his waist and another around his shoulders. Switching the light out, he headed for the spare room where a bed was always made up in case Gareth or another friend wanted to stay over.

"Jack?"

He turned towards the voice, looking at the stairwell. The downstairs hall light was on, throwing a long shadow up the stairs. The figure of a man moved slightly, the shadow seeming to turn.

"Jack?" The shadow turned again as if the figure were looking for him, the voice faint and plaintive. Slowly the dark figure slipped away, merging with the other shadows in the hall.

"Jack?" his father's voice repeated once more before the house fell silent.

2: SATURDAY

The next morning, Jack examined his bruised nose in the bathroom mirror. It was swollen slightly, and there were dark bruises beneath his eyes, but at least it didn't look broken. He smiled at himself ruefully. He'd never seen anybody's broken nose before, let alone his own, so how would he know if it was broken? He washed his face carefully, cleaned his teeth, then went to the toilet. Only then did he remember last night's episode, looking over at the shower curtain, he sighed as he remembered he'd wet the bed.

Flushing the toilet and wrapping his dressing gown around him, Jack headed for the main bedroom. Suddenly he stopped on the landing and glanced at the stairwell, remembering more than his embarrassment of last night. "Je-sus," he whispered, running his hand through his hair. He shivered and walked to his bedroom.

"Diane? It's me, Jack."

"Where the bloody ell did yew get to yesterday? Mum's bin dead worried. She thought yew were gonna stay yere."

Jack sighed and sat on the edge of his bed. He'd hoped that his sister wouldn't answer the phone, but with his dad dead and his mum probably still crying it had been a pretty slim hope. "Is Matt there?" he asked. Looking around at the clothes he'd thrown off last night, he spotted his cigarettes and lighter and tried dragging them over with his foot.

"E's not yer yet. E said e'd be up at ten." Jack glanced at the clock on the bedside table: 9:17.

"Okay, can you get him to give me a ring when he gets there?"

"Yew aven't even asked ow Mum is yet. Yew don' care, do yew?"

"Diane, will you shut up? Just get Matt to phone me."Before his sister could say anything more, Jack hung up. He reached down and shook a cigarette out of the pocket, popped it between his lips and lit it up, then strolled over to the washing basket and retrieved the dirty sheets, grimacing as his hands hit a damp patch. He carried them at arm's length out of the bedroom and down the stairs and dumped the lot in the washing machine. After sorting that out, he trotted back up to his bedroom and dressed, then hung around waiting for Matt to phone.

"What can I do you for, Jack?" his brother said.

"Are you going to be at Mum's for the day?" Jack asked.

"Pretty much. Why's that?"

"Well," said Jack, then paused, unsure of what to say, of what he wanted to say. "I guess I didn't fancy visiting if it was just going to be Diane up there," he finished lamely.

"I've got some stuff to do this evening, but I'm probably going to be here today. You going to come up?"

"Yeah, I'll be up in an hour or so. Catch you later."

"So, what happened to your face?" Matt asked as they walked from their parents' house down to the ring road that encircled the estate.

"It bumped into the toilet wall of a pub last night," Jack answered with a small laugh. They walked in silence for a minute, heading up the hill to the top of the estate. "I was in the pub last night," Jack continued, "having a piss when some guy throws me against the wall and pins me there. I seriously thought I was about to get raped, Matt. Anyway, next thing I know this bloke is holding me against the wall, telling me to cremate Dad and then forget about him." He looked over at his brother. "And forget about the Dreaming Pool."

Matt sighed, his breath frosting slightly in front of him. "Did you recognise this man?"

"Fuck, I didn't even see him, he was behind me the whole time."

"Shame. If you'd known the guy I could have had something done, found something out." Jack stopped and turned to his brother.

"You could have had something done? What the hell is that supposed to mean?"

"Exactly what it says. Had you known the man, I

could have had something done." Matt carried on walking up the hill, hands buried deep in his overcoat pockets, collar turned up against the wind. Jack followed him in silence wishing he'd worn something more substantial than his denim jacket.

"Matt?" he said eventually. "What do you do?"

"What do you mean?"

"What do you do? What's your job?I mean, in that get -up, " he said, indicating Matt's suit and tie, overcoat and gloves, all in black, "- - you look either like a copper or a gangster."

Matt laughed at him. "Nothing so dramatic, Jack.I work in insurance for a small family firm, that's all. I know a fair few people through my work and I know how to get things done."

"Like seeing the policeman in charge of Dad's murder?"

"Exactly." He stopped in his tracks and turned to Jack. "Who told you it was murder?"

"Well, no one. It was just a figure of speech." He stared at his brother. "Was Dad murdered?"

"No, I told you, they think it was a wild dog." They started walking again, Jack reaching into his jacket and taking out a packet of cigarettes. He lit one up and blew the smoke out into the cold air.

"Matt?" he said. "Getting beaten up wasn't the only thing that happened to me last night."

"What else happened?"

"I . . . I had to get up in the middle of the night, to go to the toilet. As I walked back across the hall, someone called my name from the stairs. I looked . . . and it was Dad."

"You were dreaming," Matt said simply.

"No, I wasn't. I'd just had a shower. I was wide awake. I saw a shadow on the wall and heard him call my name three times. Scared the shit out of me, I can tell you." Matt shrugged and continued walking, leaving Jack's words behind him like the smoke from Jack's cigarette. At the top of the ring road, where it levelled out before dropping back down the other side of the estate, Matt stopped and looked up at the rest of the hill, covered in trees that stood dead and bare in the middle of October. A light drizzle hung in the air, not falling so much as being pushed around by the wind, obscuring their view of the hill's summit.

"Fancy taking a walk?" Matt asked, pointing across the road. Opposite them was the entrance to a lane, the tarmac of the road giving way to a rock -strewn path that disappeared into the woods and mist.

"Is that the way to the Pool?"

Matt nodded and crossed the road, looking back at his brother when he stood in the lane's mouth. "You coming or what?" he called. Jack stepped off the pavement, looked both ways and walked across the road to where his brother stood.

"Won't it be guarded or something?" Jack asked.

"In this weather?" Matt asked, walking off into the lane, Jack following him. "No, it'll have some police tape around it and that'll be it, I'd imagine."

Together the brothers walked through the drizzle that covered everything in a fine silver sheen, reflecting the small amount of sunlight that filtered through the dull, leaden clouds above. It had been just over twenty years since Jack had been down this lane, and he wondered whether it had really changed that much in the intervening years. His memories from his last visit centred more on the nightmarish events in the Pool itself than on the journey there, so he had no way of comparing this lane with that of his childhood.

"I'm going to ruin my shoes doing this," Matt said. He stood at a sty on the left side of the lane which led into a large field that seemed to be nothing more than a huge puddle filled with thick red mud.

"We could always come back tomorrow or next week or something," Jack said.

"You're going to be okay," Matt said and pointed at Jack's Dr Martens, then at his own shoes. "These things cost a bomb." With that, he climbed over and gingerly stepped into the mud patch, walking off towards the woods that lay on the opposite side. Running his hands through his hair in exasperation, Jack followed, trudging after his brother in much the same way he had all those years before.

A small overgrown path wound through the woods. By the time they had forced their way through more trees and undergrowth than Jack had seen in years, he was breathing hard, coughing slightly with almost every other breath. He was immeasurably happy when he felt hard, flat stone beneath his feet and stepped out on to a small paved area that marked the edge of a clearing.

"Bring back any memories, Jack?" Matt asked, holding his arm out, indicating the large empty Pool before them. Jack stepped forward, up to the edge, and looked at the bottom, clearly visible now due to the lack of water. Like coral, regular bumps and nodules that looked treacherous to walk upon covered the floor, each one having a metallic sheen: gold here, silver there, copper somewhere else, dull in places but blindingly bright in others where the small amount of sunlight caught it. He found his gaze being drawn to the corner where his panic attack or whatever it was had happened. It looked no different to the rest of the place. "It must have been drained at some point," Matt said as he walked along the side of the Pool to the opposite end. Hunkering down, he picked something up.

"What is it?" Jack asked. Matt turned and held up a strip of fluorescent yellow tape with POLICE printed repeatedly on it.

"This must have been where they found him."

Slowly, Jack walked around and joined his brother. Looking down he saw a bare patch in the thick grass and brambles, littered with more tape. In some places the tape was still tied to three or four wooden pegs driven into the earth, marking out a rough rectangle. Jack lit up another cigarette and the pair of them stood and looked down at their father's last resting place.

"It's kind of strange to think of him being dead," Jack said. Matt turned to him.

"You haven't spoken to him for years. What the hell would you care?"

"Hey, he was still my dad too, remember? We may not have talked for -- "

"No, Jack. You hadn't talked for years. I was still in touch with him and Mum. Do you know how many times they asked me for your telephone number? How many times they wanted me to tell them where you lived, or even just to arrange some sort of meeting with you in Newport? But I couldn't, because you'd made me promise not to. I was caught between the proverbial rock and a hard place. Thing is, it was worse because it was my family and my brother. You've caused me fuck knows how much hassle over the last few years and I've never even been thanked for it. Now this happens and you just stand there and say how strange it is."

"Yeah, I think it's pretty strange, Matt. I think it's damn fucking weird how Dad gets killed by the side of a pool we visited years ago and how a few days later, I get beaten up in a pub and told to forget about it. Then I either dream about Dad or the bastard's ghost visits me, yet I'm the one who hasn't talked with him for fucking years. Yeah, I think it's strange. How come you didn't get beaten up? How come you didn't get haunted? Eh? If you're so in tune with the family, if you spent all that time with them, how comes it was me who got all the shit?"

The two brothers stared at each other, their breath steaming in the thin drizzle between them. At some point during the last minute they had stepped closer to each other, facing off in the dull grey air.

"It's always about you, isn't it?" Matt said. "You never stop to think that maybe Mum's been hassled by the same guy, or that maybe Diane's had a visit from someone threatening her, do you? You're just worried about your precious little self. You don't give a fuck about anyone else."

"That's not true." Even to his own ears, the cry sounded petulant.

"Isn't it? Did you think about Mum or Diane, or even me, after you got beaten up? Did you?" Jack threw his cigarette into the Pool, and turned away from his brother. "You see what I mean? For what it's worth, neither Mum nor Diane have seen anyone except friends and neighbours. But you weren't the only one to get a visitor last night."

Jack looked back at him. "*You* did?" Matt nodded tersely. "Why didn't you tell me earlier?"

"Because I can look after myself."

"I see. So now it's a big-brother-looking-after-me sort of thing, is it? *You* can help me, but *I* can't help you, right?"

"Which one of us has spoken with the police? Which one of us is trying to get to the bottom of this thing? While you were off getting pissed with your mates, I was working."

Jack stared at him, in his overcoat and round specs, his crew cut glistening with the rain upon it and wondered how his brother viewed him. Then without another word, Jack turned and walked back along the path, heading for the field, the lane and home.

"Hey, Jack. Good timing."

Jack looked up as he approached the car park behind his mother's house and saw Rachel Lewis standing beside her own vehicle, with a raincoat covering her suit and an umbrella open above her head. She frowned as he stepped nearer, noting his bruised face and the mud covering his jeans. "Jesus, what happened to you? You look like shit," she said.

"Thanks. I thought you were going to call me?"

"I was. I am, I mean. Thing is . . . " She trailed off, looking vaguely embarrassed.

"Let me guess: boyfriend?"

Rachel nodded. "Well, for now anyway." Jack looked at her, reaching for another of his cigarettes. She shrugged, half smiling at him. "I'm kinda preparing his P45, if you know what I mean."

Jack nodded, grinning as he lit up his smoke. "Listen, you wanna sit indoors or something? I'm wet enough as it is."

She looked over at his mother's house. "Unless you've got a key we're stuck out here. Nobody's in. We could sit in my car, though," she offered. As they headed for it, however, she stopped. "Hang on; your feet are filthy. Let's sit in your car. I don't know you well enough to foot the cleaning bill, if you'll pardon the pun."

A moment later they were sitting in Jack's car, with his window wound down slightly to allow the cigarette smoke to drift out, the engine running and the heater on.

"Well, you were certainly full of more conversation yesterday," Rachel said after they had sat in silence for a while.

"Sorry," Jack said, running his hand through his hair. "I just had an argument with Matt, my brother." He looked over at her. "Not really conducive to being witty."

"What was it about?"

He sighed. "My Dad. Our Dad, whatever. You know I haven't really been in touch with my family over the last few years? Well, I never realised how much that pissed Matt off. I'd made him promise to never tell Mum or Dad where I lived or anything and it came as a bit of a shock to have him tell me they'd wanted to get in touch for years. I kind of thought they'd have gotten bored and forgotten about me."

"As you did about them?"

"I suppose so." He unwound the window further and flicked the remains of his cigarette out into the car park. "Now I just feel crappy. Angry at Matt, angry at myself. Sorry that my Dad's dead and that I've no chance of telling him to his face."

"You could always tell your mum that. She'd probably love to hear it, the state she's in."

"Yeah, I know." Jack sighed and flicked the windscreen wipers on for a second, giving them a quick, blurred image of his mother's house as if they were both looking at it through the same teary eyes. "Matt reckons I'm self - centred, that I never think of anybody apart from myself." Rachel shrugged noncommittally, making him grin. "Hey, come on, this is the point where you're supposed to say no, you're not, Jack."

"Once again, Mr Bradley, I don't know you well enough. For all I know you could be a self -centred, obnoxious bastard." She smiled at him.

"You could have stopped after 'I don't know you well enough'. That would have done just fine." They stared at each other, smiling through the silence.

"How did you get the bruise?" Rachel said after a moment, indicating his nose. It was his turn to shrug.

"Some guy punched me last night. Or rather he bounced me off the toilet wall face-first."

"Hmm. Do I really want to go for a drink with some guy who gets into pub fights, I ask myself?"

"It wasn't a pub fight,"Jack said. He told her about his adventures the night before, but only those that took place in the pub. If he was going to go out and have a drink with her, he reasoned, the last thing she needed to know about was him was that he had been haunted by his recently deceased father. Or had wet the bed.

"Have you been to the police?" Rachel asked once he was finished. Jack shook his head. "What about back to the pub? Maybe the landlord or the bar staff know the bloke or saw something?"

Jack looked at her, a smile inching its way across his face. "Rachel, you're a genius. The pub's got security cameras and I know the landlord. I just hope he had them recording last night. You are brilliant. I could kiss you for thinking of that."

She looked at him for a second. "So why don't you?"

Jack leaned across, reaching out and gently pulling her closer, kissing her softly on the lips. He watched her as she closed her eyes and kissed him back, her hint of perfume making him uncomfortably aware of the smell of his cigarettes. Tentatively, her tongue peeped out from between her teeth and licked at his lips, encouraging his response.
He stroked the side of her face as their kiss continued, running his fingers slowly through her hair and around her ear, slipping down on to her neck.

With a sigh, Rachel broke the kiss, pecking him once more on the lips and smiling into his eyes. They sat in the same position for a minute until Jack moved back, still staring at her.

"So do we get to have that drink, then?" he asked.

"Sure." She glanced down at her watch. "I've gotta get back to work."

Jack scrabbled about in his denim jacket pockets, looking for a pen and paper. "Here," Rachel said, handing him a small notepad and a pen from her own jacket.

"I'm not sure how you were going to ring me without

this," Jack said, writing his number down.

"I could have gotten it from your mother. I'm a friend of the family, remember?" Jack passed her the pad and pen back and she put them away.

"Is this where the slightly embarrassed silence comes in?" he asked with a grin.

"Nope," Rachel said, opening the door and stepping out. She leaned back in and said, "It comes after I tell you that I'll give you a ring either tonight or tomorrow, and when we do go out for that drink --" she added with a wink at him, " -- bring some mints or something. I like you Jack but I don't fancy kissing a man who tastes like an ashtray." She quickly blew a kiss at his stunned face and closed the door, walking over to her own car, waving once before she drove away.

"Cheeky cow," Jack said quietly, unsure of how he should react, but unable to stop smiling all the same.
As he sat in his car, he noticed Matt standing off to one side watching him and found himself wondering how long he'd been there.

Jack drove back to Newport, parked his car outside his house and walked up to his local pub. The barmaid greeted him by name and poured him a pint without his having to ask for one. "Is Dave around?" he asked as he sipped at his beer.

A minute or two later the landlord appeared behind the bar; he was a tall thin man whose large beer gut seemed out of place, sitting above his belt line as if he had a football stuffed up his shirt.

"Hello, Jack. What can I do for you?"

"This might seem like a strange question, but did you have your cameras working last night?"

The landlord chuckled. "Why, you want to get a look at the guy who thumped you?"

"Is it that obvious?"

"With a fucked-up nose like yours it's hardly surprising." He paused to pour himself a half pint of lager.
"After the hassle I had with the police last year, of course my cameras were fucking working." Jack nodded in un-

derstanding; the year before his local had unintentionally staged the largest pub fight Newport had seen for several years . While no one had actually been charged, Dave had borne the brunt of the brewery's frustration, having to pay for a closed- circuit security system in an attempt to prevent the same thing happening again.

"I don't suppose there's any chance of having a look at last night's tape, is there?" Jack asked.

"Seeing as it's you," Dave said, walking to the end of the bar and lifting up the flap, "let's see what we can do for you." As they walked up to the landlord's office, he said, "I must admit, I'm surprised at you getting into a fight."

"It wasn't really a fight, though," Jack said.
For the third time that day he explained roughly what had happened, though he left out his attacker's comments concerning his family and the Dreaming Pool. "So I don't know what the hell it was about, mate."

Dave chuckled to himself and led Jack into his office, where a computer monitor and TV and video sat, surrounded by a mass of paperwork, invoices, half -drunk mugs of tea and overflowing ashtrays. "Sit yourself down," he said, indicating the spare chair. "You're lucky I don't turn the thing on during the day," he said as he rewound the videocassette that was in the recorder. "Otherwise the bloody thing would have been taped over by now."

"You're an angel," Jack said dryly, lighting up a cigarette and offering one to Dave.

"Cheers."

When the tape finished rewinding, Dave pressed the play button, then began to fast-forward through the black and white images that flickered on the screen. After the previous year's near -riot, which had started in the gents' toilets, the landlord always had one camera pointed at the entrance to them and it was this view that he scanned through.

"About what time did it happen?" he asked.

"Roughly half ten. Not long before closing time, anyway." Jack watched as people entered and left the toilets in fast motion, faces rushing by as the beers they had drunk took effect. "Whoa!" he exclaimed. "Run it from there."

Dave stopped the video, rewound it a minute or so,

then played it. Silently the pair watched as a monochrome version of Jack entered the toilets. A moment later, looking out of place in the mainly student-oriented bar, a black man wearing a dark suit followed him in. Nobody else entered the gents' for a full two minutes until the man whom Jack recognised as the one who had called him a shirt lifter went in. Not long after, the coloured man walked back out. Fifty-three seconds later, according to the timer on the video, Jack himself stumbled out, his face obviously the worse for wear.

"There's your fella," Dave said, rewinding the tape to the point at which the black man had left the toilets. The pair of them stared at the screen. All they could really see of him was his forehead and his scalp, covered sparsely with hair-- hardly enough for a positive identification. "You want me to save this tape? Give it to the cops?" Dave asked him.

Jack sighed, blowing out a plume of smoke. "No, it's all alright. It's not as if we could actually use that as evidence of anything. I mean, I never even saw the guy who did it." He stared at the screen nonetheless, trying to get some sort of impression of the man's face.

"He could be fucking anyone for all we know," Dave shrugged. "Sorry we couldn't do more. You in here tonight?"

"Yeah, should be," Jack said as he stood, gulping at his beer. "Cheers Dave, catch you later."

"The twentieth century has seen more activity from secret societies than any other period in history. It's a fact that the Masons, and the Illuminati especially, are gearing up to something big happening at the end of the millennium."

"Oh come on, Camilla, you can't really believe that?" Gareth downed the remains of his beer and looked across the table at the earnest speaker. Jack smiled at her, partly in sympathy.

"I'm serious," she said, flicking her long blonde hair away from her face and waving her arms as she talked, the puffy sleeves of her fancy blouse looking like half- inflated hot air balloons. "At the end of this millennium, when everybody else is out getting drunk, the leaders of the Illuminati will all be gathered by the pyramids in Egypt, ushering in their own age when they'll take even more control of the governments of the world."

"Why?" Kate asked, dragging on her cigarette.
Of all Jack's friends, she was the most vociferous in refuting Camilla's theories of a secret world order mainly because of, even though she denied it, her own Christian beliefs.

"Oh come on, Kate," Camilla said. "Whoever runs the governments runs the world. It's obvious."

"But surely the people run the governments?" Annie said shyly. She was a friend of Camilla's from school who had recently moved back to Newport.

"She's got a point," Kate said, "or is democracy some thing that passed you by?"

"Democracy? What on earth makes you think any government is elected by the people? Every single election, especially in the Western world, is run and managed by the ruling elite, which in turn is made up of Master Masons, high ranking members of the Illuminati and the Rosicrucians. The thought that -- "

"Hey, hang on," Jack interrupted. "This is getting a little out of hand, here. You have to admit, Camilla, the idea of secret societies running things from behind the lines is a little far -fetched."

She smiled at him. "That is exactly what they want you to think." Gareth and Kate groaned as their friend grinned triumphantly. Jack shook his head, grinning as he stubbed out his cigarette in the ashtray. "They control the media. They can release exactly what they want and use it to discredit those who know the truth. You know about Roswell, yeah?" Everybody nodded. "Nothing happened there. Nothing at all."

"But what about the newspaper reports at the time?" Annie asked.

"Lies," Camilla said. "The entire thing was a distraction from what was happening in Washington at the same time."

"What the fuck are you talking about?" Kate asked. She and Camilla had been friends for several years, but when Camilla started on her conspiracy theories, Kate found it difficult to remember that friendship.

"Where's the best place to hide a book? In a library." Camilla looked around at the four of them. "What is the basis of any illusion? You make people look at one hand while you do something else with the other. Roswell was deliberately constructed and has been purposefully followed up throughout the years, purely as a way of distracting any serious investigation away from the real alien landings that happened outside Washington in 1947. Jack? Where're you going?" she asked as he stood up opposite her.

"Just getting a beer for me and Gareth." He picked up the few empty glasses and carried them over to the bar, ordering his drinks when the barmaid noticed him. As he waited for them to be poured he glanced around the pub, wondering if he would be able to spot the coloured man in the suit, but the place, as usual, was full of students.

"Looking for anyone in particular?" Kate asked at his elbow. He shrugged and smiled.

"No, not really."

Kate ordered her own drinks as the barmaid delivered Jack's. "Camilla really gets on my nerves when she starts on about all these bloody conspiracy things," Kate said.

"Well, you know, each to their own and all that. I kind of enjoy some of her theories, but I think she just takes it too seriously, you know?"

"Jesus, don't let Camilla hear you say you enjoy 'em. You'll never get rid of her. Here, Jack? Is it my imagination or is Annie taking an interest in Gareth?" Jack looked over at the table where Camilla was still holding court. Annie sat next to her and, unless Jack was mistaken, she was definitely sneaking long looks at Gareth. He turned back to Kate.

"It's possible," he admitted.

"I just hope she doesn't end up like poor Tara," Kate said with an embarrassed smile. Jack laughed, picked up his and Gareth's drinks and took them back over to the table where Camilla was educating their friends about the Masonic signs and slogans dotted around the American one-dollar bill.

"Everybody knows that stuff about the dollar bill, Camilla." Jack said as he lit up another cigarette.

"Everybody knows it, but not everybody believes it, even though the evidence is right in front of their eyes!"

"Do you really believe every single Freemason is part of some global conspiracy? All the ones I know of seem to spend all their time getting pissed."

"I don't believe *every single* Mason is in on the conspiracy," Camilla said carefully, making her point, "but neither do I believe *every single* Mason spends his time getting pissed."

"Well, you didn't waste any time." Jack looked back over his shoulder at the speaker and saw the girl he had picked up at the party a couple of days ago, the one who had been sleeping in his bed when his mother had phoned in the middle of the night, the one who had come over all serious the following morning, the one whose name he couldn't for the life of him remember. She looked over at Camilla, noting her good looks and long blonde hair, and sneered. "Going for bimbos now, are you Jack?"

Jack stood up and faced her. "Camilla's a friend of mine. What's it got to do with you?"

"Oh, fine, just forget about what happened between us," she said, actually stamping her foot.

"Well, I've forgotten your name, so I'm halfway there," Jack said, and the next instant was wearing whatever it was that Eve (that was her name, Jack realised) was drinking because she threw the contents of her tall glass into his face before turning around and storming off. Various people stared and laughed at Jack as he watched her leave, his cigarette hanging limp and wet from his mouth. He dropped it on the floor and sat back down.

"Another great Bradley romance over with?" Kate asked. She had reached the table in time to see the floor show and was quietly smiling at him as he sat down. He chuckled, wiped his face with the sleeve of his shirt and lit up another cigarette. "God, a one night stand and she thinks I'm going to marry her."

"She's probably after your money, Jack." Camilla said.

"I think she's very nice, actually," Gareth said rather seriously. The other four looked at him and burst into laughter.

"So any of you guys want to come back for a cuppa or something?" Jack asked as they all stood outside the pub. Around them, other drinkers were wandering home or standing about, some talking as Jack and his friend were. One or two couples were kissing, heedless of either the light rain or the catcalls of others.

"Not for me, Jack. I've gotta get up for work in the morning," Kate said.

"I'm going to head off home too," Camilla said. "Another night, eh Jack?"

"Annie?"

"No thanks, I'm staying at Cam's house tonight."

"What about you, Gareth?" Jack asked him. Gareth looked from Jack to the three girls who were just moving away.

"I'll catch you later," Gareth said and ran after Kate, Camilla and Annie, intent on walking them home even though they lived about two miles apart. Jack laughed at his friend and buttoned up his denim jacket. Lighting another cigarette, he turned in the opposite direction and walked the short distance home.

He unlocked his front door with a hand that was shaking from more than just the cold. The walk home through the cold, wet and dark streets had unnerved Jack more than he would have thought possible. Images of his dead father kept springing to mind, and he expected to see his dad's shade beneath every lamp post, and around every corner; and when he didn't, he merely became more convinced that it would be around the next corner or under the next lamp post. So it went on until he reached his front door; rattling the key in the lock, he promised himself that on no account would he even glance at the landing on the stairs where the shadow had appeared. He would step inside, make himself a quick cup of tea or glass of squash and then go to bed.

As soon as he was inside, he stared up at the landing. There was nothing there.

"Thank Christ for that," he whispered and closed the door. He took his jacket off and hung it on the banister, running his hands through his hair as he walked into the kitchen. After turning on the light he placed a glass on the counter and rummaged in another cupboard for the bottle of squash.

He jumped as the glass hit the floor, smashing into tiny pieces. Jack stared at the remains for a moment, thinking that he hadn't placed it securely enough on the counter, that it had obviously slid off the edge. As he watched, a cup rolled from the draining rack beside the sink and tumbled to the floor, adding its shards to those of the glass.

"Oh Christ," Jack muttered before pandemonium descended upon his kitchen. Cups leaped from the sink and the counters, crashing to the floor; glasses shot across the table, launching themselves briefly into the air before hitting the ground; every plate on the draining rack split cleanly into two with a series of sharp snaps; plastic jars of herbs and spices exploded, spilling their aromatic guts over the kitchen surfaces; the single bulb blew out with a pop, showering Jack with thin, hot glass and leaving him illuminated only by the street light outside his house; the table and chairs began to lift and fall, banging their legs on the floor; the cupboards joined them as if at the behest of some mad conductor, their doors opening and slamming shut continously; finally every door in the house joined in the chorus, the noise rising to a huge level, reducing Jack to a quivering ball in the corner, his hands over his ears, his eyes squeezed shut.

Everything stopped.

Jack stared at the devastation that his kitchen had suffered and wondered if he had gone mad. The only noise now was his own breathing, the rise and fall of his chest bringing the scent of mixed herbs and spices to his assaulted senses. Then the footsteps started.

He stared at the closed kitchen door as, from behind it, huge, echoing footsteps sounded. Something was walking down the stairs. But the stairs are carpeted, Jack thought wildly, chuckling madly to himself as the walker came to the bottom and stepped into the hall. The footsteps paused for a second, then slowly, deliberately, they headed for the kitchen. Jack tried to ease himself further into the corner that he had sheltered in, his gaze never leaving the door as the footsteps came to a halt behind it.

The handle turned and the door opened a couple of inches.

"**Jack?**" His father's voice drifted into the room on a plume of grey smoke. "**Jack?**"

Hiding in his corner, Jack stayed silent.

"**Don't make me come in there, Jack.**" His voice was no longer lost and pleading as it had been the night before. Now it was strong and purposeful and Jack could almost hear a cold smile hidden behind the words.

"What . . . what do you want?"

There was a pause, and Jack wondered whether he'd done the wrong thing by answering.

"I want to know who murdered me, Jack. I need to know who killed me."

A moment later the door was closed softly, leaving Jack alone in the dimly lit room amidst the wreckage.

3: SUNDAY

The town centre of Caerphilly had been overhauled since Jack had wandered through it as a child, yet all the modernisation, pedestrianisation and attempts at civilisation couldn't change the dismal ex-miner's town where he had grown up. The new shopping centre; just next to a new petrol station which was just next to another old council estate, made no difference to Jack's mind. The just lain paving stones and wide open spaces, flanked by sparkling new shops with their gleaming plastic and steel, merely looked out of place. The buildings seemed to invite the gangs of surly youths who hung around the centre to take up arms amidst a sea of trolleys and wreak havoc.

Kicking his way through the litter and patches of chewing gum, Jack made his way past the few Sunday shoppers who were taking advantage of their council's initiative. He wondered how many of them realised that the idea of blocking off roads and turning them into pedestrian areas was hardly new and certainly not unique to Caerphilly; probably not that many. When he had been thirteen or so and still in touch with a couple of friends from Caerphilly, he had been amazed to find out how many of them had never been to Cardiff. He doubted that the people here would know that the capital had been pedestrianised first, with Newport quickly following suit; then, like some bizarre Welsh valley's domino effect, the trend had spread to Caerphilly and Abergavenny and Ponty-God-knows-where.

Depressed, Jack trudged up the hill past the cenotaph, the castle sprawling over to his right, huge, grey and silent. He had visited the massive stone monster so many times as a child that now it was merely something else to feel sad about. When he was younger, the castle had seemed full of mystery and wonder, as if knights in armour might come galloping across the drawbridge at any moment. Now it just looked like an old castle, wounded in battle, collapsed and near death. Jack could never remember whether it was the second or third largest castle in Britain or in all of Europe, but he knew that, besides Caerphilly cheese, it was the one thing the town was famous for.

The Green Lady hotel was a small, squat building with curtains that looked as if they had been hung in the year of the Queen's coronation, then drawn and quartered at regular intervals. Jack wondered whether the owner of the hotel knew what a washing machine looked like. As he stepped inside the dark, musty hallway, dust motes flew up into the air, with his every step dancing in the few beams of sunlight that pierced the gloom.

"Hiya," the woman behind the counter said half-heartedly as he stepped up. She was a big woman with a round face that belied the notion that all fat people are jolly; the single dark eyebrow that ran across her brow knotted into a frown almost hiding the tiny eyes that glared out at him from behind the thick lenses of her black- rimmed glasses.

"Hi. Is Matt Bradley here?" The woman swivelled around on her seat and looked at an old-fashioned pigeon-hole box nailed to the wall. She reached one small, fat hand out and groped about in one of the holes, then spun back to face Jack, her earrings jangling wildly.

"Is key's not yer, so he must be in, then?" she said, turning the statement into a question.

"Which room is he in?" Jack asked. Having argued with his sister Diane on the phone that morning, trying to get Matt's address from her, Jack had no desire to listen to another Caerphilly accent. Fortunately, the woman spared him and just gave him the room number and directions, staring after him as he walked up the stairs.

Standing in front of the door to Matt's room, Jack paused, wondering how his brother would react to his arrival. Only one way to find out, he thought, and rapped on the door.

"You're early," Matt said as he opened it, then stared in astonishment at Jack who stood looking vaguely embarrassed. "I was expecting someone else," Matt said as he quickly regained his composure. He stood aside and let Jack in. "What are you doing here?"

Jack shrugged. "I guess I wanted to apologise about yesterday. Maybe I was selfish all those years and I know I never really knew what you did for me, telling Mum and Dad all those things about -- "

"Yeah, okay, Jack. Apology accepted. Let's not turn it

into an Oscar speech, eh?" Matt looked at his younger brother from where he stood next to the still open door. "Is that it?"

"Well, yeah."

"Like I said, I'm expecting somebody and, if it's all the same to you, I'd rather you weren't here when they turned up." Jack stared at him, trying to find a joke laying behind his words, humour playing around his eyes, but there was nothing.

"You're serious?"

Matt smiled slightly. "Yes. I'm serious. Goodbye, Jack. I'll see you at Mum's at some point, or maybe at the funeral. It's been arranged for Wednesday, by the way, at three o'clock." He held the door for him and closed it as soon as Jack left.

Walking down the stairs, Jack couldn't help but feel a little hurt and confused. He and his brother had argued the day before and, when he had tried to apologise, Matt had said thanks and goodbye in less than a minute. He walked through the dim, dusty foyer and out the door, holding it open for another man who was entering just as he left. Stepping down to the pavement, Jack stopped short and quickly glanced back at the door to the hotel.

The man he had just passed, whom he had held the door for . . . it was the black man from the pub, the one who had beaten him up in the toilets on Friday.

He trotted back up the steps and looked through the glass of the door. Dimly, he saw the man walking up the stairs. It could have been anyone, of course. Anyone at all.

Jack walked back into the hotel, ignoring the reception ist's puzzled look, and took the stairs two at a time, as quietly as possible. Reaching the top, he looked left and saw the black guy stepping inside Matt's room. "Well, fuck me,"he whispered. Creeping into the corridor and along to his brother's apartment, he looked around a couple of times. Seeing and hearing no one, Jack bent down and put his eye to the keyhole of the door.

"You wouldn't believe how close you've just come Peter," Matt said as he walked from one side of the room to another, in and out of Jack's limited field of vision." M y brother just decided to pay me a visit and apologise for the argument we had yesterday."

"You're kidding me?" Jack was pretty sure it was the voice he had heard whispering into his ear on Friday night, but its owner was out of sight.

"No, I'm not. Chances are you missed him by a matter of seconds." There was silence for a moment or two, then the other man, Peter, asked what Jack had been wearing. "Denim jacket, jeans. Usual stuff." said Matt The second man laughed, a clucking cackle that reminded Jack of Sid James. "What's so funny?"

"He just held the front door open for me. Didn't look at me twice." Peter said. The pair of them had a good laugh at Jack's expense and despite himself, Jack could feel his cheeks burning, humiliated that his brother was laughing at him with this other man. Eventually, they calmed down and Jack heard the popping of cans and something, presumably beer, being poured into glasses.

"The funeral's on Wednesday, by the way," Matt said, "so we can move on the Pool on Friday night for certain."

"Great. Who's head of the Chapel up this way?"

"Detective Inspector Martin, coincidentally the policeman in charge of the investigation into my father's murder," Matt said, and Jack could hear the grin in his voice. "There should be no problems at the Dreaming Pool, either; because he hasn't made a big fuss and closed the entire area off, everybody assumes that whatever happened up there is over and done with."

"Whereas if he'd done the opposite . . ."

"The place would be crawling with kids, reporters and assorted nosy bastards for weeks. No, D.I. Martin's done a good job, I must admit."

"What the bloody hell are yew up to, then?" the receptionist said from the top of the stairs. Jack snapped his head around to her, then quickly back to the keyhole where Matt's large form had appeared, standing in the middle of his room, obviously alerted by the noise. Jack stood and ran down the corridor, ignoring the woman's cries of "'Ere!" as he charged down the stairs, one hand holding the banister, the other held out for balance. In seconds, he was out the front door and running down the hill, heading for his car.

Jack sat in his car, a cigarette in one hand, and a can of Pepsi in the other, waiting for Rachel to finish work. From the large, low building in front of him, a procession of black-clad mourners filed out into the waiting drizzle, the weather coming out in sympathy with their feelings. To Jack's way of thinking, on the other hand, the weather merely reinforcing the fact that the world didn't care about you or your loss; there was no pot of gold at the end of the rainbow and no sunshine through the clouds after you'd buried (cremated his mind insisted) your loved one. It always rained at funerals - it was a law of nature. It was the world laughing at you for believing that you or anyone you cared for mattered in the slightest.

Jack sat up as Rachel stepped out on to the porch, an umbrella held above her head. Following her was an older man, his bald head gleaming in the pale light from the sign that hung over the door proclaiming the building as belonging to Navvarro & Son Funeral Directors, and he wondered whether that was old man Navarro or one of the sons. Rachel and the bald man stood either side of the door and helped out an old lady who clutched walking sticksin both hands, her knuckles swollen and red, her black dress and hat blowing gently in the slight wind. Somehow, she climbed out and was half helped, half carried over to one of the waiting black cars. A few minutes later and the rest of the friends and relatives of the the dead person had leaked out of the building, allowing Jack to climb out of his own car, pitching his cigarette into the wind and jogging over to the crematorium.

"Sorry, sir, we're - Jack?" Rachel looked at him as he stood just inside the doors, his scruffy jeans and jacket out of place amidst the solemn surroundings.

"What are you doing here?"

"Is there somewhere we can talk?" he said, his voice lowered automatically, instantly feeling the pressure that only libraries, churches and places of the dead could exert on the vocal chords.

"I finish in about fifteen minutes." The bald headed man stepped out into the foyer

"Is everything alright, Rachel?" "Yes thanks, Mr Navarro. This is Jack Bradley. His father's ceremony is on Wednesday." she said quickly.

"My sincerest sympathies, Mr Bradley," the man said, stepping forward and taking Jack's hand even before he could offer it. "We shall do our best for you and your family, you have my word."

"Thank you, Mr Navarro." Jack managed. For some bizarre reason, he found himself fighting back an attack of giggles, triggered by the conversation he had heard outside his brother's room and this man's fake sympathy.

"If you want to wait here, Jack," Rachel said, indicating one of the four seats against the wall, "I should be finished in a few minutes." As she left, Mr Navarro smiled at Jack and followed her, leaving Jack to sit down and wait. He stared idly at the few certificates and paintings that were dotted around the walls, then out at the bad weather, wondering whether it would rain on the day of his father's funeral, then smiled as he recalled his earlier thought. Of course it would; it was a law of nature, after all.

"Sorry to keep you waiting," Rachel said as she stepped out into the foyer fifteen minutes later, glancing at her watch. "What can I do for you?"

"Can I drive you home? I need to talk to someone."

She looked at him, frowning. "You don't look so good. What's wrong?"

"Like I said, I need to talk. Can I give you a lift?"

"I've got my car out the back. Follow me back to my place."

The drive through the worsening rain was long and slow. Jack wanted to find the person who had invented the term "rush hour" and put him in a traffic jam that didn't move for close on half an hour in the pissing rain with only a banal local radio station to listen to. Eventually, he pulled up behind Rachel's car which was opposite the comprehensive school he had attended for one term only before his parents had uprooted and moved everyone down to Newport. Pulling his jacket collar up around his neck, he quickly followed Rachel along the road and into her house.

"Nice place," he said, looking around at the exposed plaster work and peeling wallpaper.

"You can always sit out in the rain,"she said, dropping her umbrella in the stand next to the coat rack. "It was going cheap, and it's only the downstairs that's falling to bits. The upstairs is fine." She walked straight past the stairs and went down the hall, turning when he didn't follow her. "Put your jacket on the rack and come and have a cuppa."

The dining room and kitchen were in much the same state as the hall; most of the walls didn't have any wallpaper and one of them, the outside wall of the dining room, seemed to be made purely of breeze-blocks and cement draped with plastic sheeting. There were no carpets, although the kitchen floor had been covered with linoleum; still judging by its condition, Jack thought it might have been put in place just after the crucifixion.

"I was doing some work in the dining room last night," Rachel said when he asked why she kept the tea-making things down here. "I work better with a cup of tea to hand." She busied herself with kettle and teapot, asking him whether he took milk or sugar, and a few minutes later proffered him a mug filled with steaming tea. "Upstairs," she said, walking past him and heading for the hall again. Like a lost lamb, he followed her up to the first floor and into the room facing out over the street, which she had turned into a living room.

"You're right," Jack said as he looked around. "There is a difference." Here everything was colour-coordinated: carpet, curtains, sofa and chairs, even the cushions. Watercolour landscapes hung on the walls and a tasteful gas fire nestled beneath a mantelpiece which was lightly dotted with a few small ornaments and a delicate vase of dried flowers.

"Do you always take so much notice of people's

houses?" Rachel asked as she watched him take everything in. He smiled.

"Sorry. My place is a bit bare compared with most of my friends' houses. I kinda have a stereo, TV and a load of books and that's about it." He sat on the sofa, arranging a couple of cushions behind him as Rachel slipped off her shoes and sat in one of the chairs, tucking her legs up underneath her.

"So what was so important that you couldn't wait for me to ring you and ask you out?" she said. He sighed, put his cup of tea on the floor and ran both his hands through his hair.

"I went to visit my brother today," he said, taking a cigarette out of his packet.

"Sorry, Jack. No smoking in my house." He stopped and looked over at her. She smiled, shaking her head. Sighing again, he replaced it and put the packet back in the pocket of his shirt.

"I went to visit my brother today," he repeated, picking his tea up and making a show of reluctantly having to settle for that. "Like I said, we had a row yesterday and I wanted to apologise. He heard me say sorry, then basically threw me out."

"I thought you got on with your brother?" Rachel asked.

"Yeah, me too. Thing is, as I was leaving, I saw the guy who beat me up in the pub the other night, going up to visit my brother."

"Are you sure?"

"Yep. I followed him up the stairs and saw him go into my brother's room." Jack smiled as he went out. "I knelt outside his door and looked through the keyhole, spying on the pair of them. I only overheard a few bits and pieces, but it seems my brother is somehow involved in my father's death."

"What?"

Jack shook his head slowly. "I know...crazy, huh? Thing is, he told this guy Peter that my dad was murdered not that a wild dog killed him which is what he told me. Plus he knows the inspector in charge of my dad's case and it sounded as if all three of them, my brother, this guy

Peter and the inspector were all in some sort of club like the Freemasons or something. Matt said the inspector was head of some sort of chapel."

"You're not joking about this?" Rachel asked.

Jack shook his head again. "Have you heard of the Dreaming Pool?"

"The what?"

"Behind the council estate where I used to live and where my parents now live," Jack began, giving Rachel a potted history of the strange pool that sat in the woods only a few miles from the town. He told her of his father's death there, his own experience of almost drowning one summer and of the small boy who had been killed there only a matter of weeks afterward. He talked about the strange liquid that had filled the pool and he wondered whether it had really been water. He even mentioned the children's belief that you could not visit the pool unless you had dreamed of it first. Before he was even aware of it, he was telling Rachel of the past two nights when he had been visited, haunted, by his father; he spoke of the first sighting, that may well have been induced by alcohol and suppressed grief, then of the previous night's unmistakable terror in the kitchen.

"My dad told me that he was murdered before I heard Matt say anything about it," Jack said, his cup of tea cold and forgotten in his lap. "Matt told me some sort of animal had killed him and that the police were looking for a wild dog or something. A couple of days later my dad's ghost turns up and tells me to find out who killed him. Christ, that sounds fucking ridiculous when you say it out loud."

"So what are you going to do?" she said with a grin. "How are you going to find your dad's killer? Does Matt know that you know he's somehow connected? Since when has a policeman been in charge of a chapel? What's so special about this Dreaming Pool and what's going to happen there on Friday?"

Jack looked at her and smiled for the first time since he had begun talking about the Pool.

"You ought to be hosting a bloody quiz show," he said. He suddenly put his cup on the floor and stood up.

"Let's go up there. To the Pool."

"What, now?"

"Why not?"

Rachel looked out the window behind her. "Well, because it's still raining for one thing." She turned back to him. "And there's no way I'm going to get filthy clambering through muddy fields and woods just to visit some empty pool." She looked at her watch. "Plus it'll be dark by the time we get there." Jack stood smiling at her, hands in his pockets, his eyes bright. Rachel sighed and placed her own cup on the floor. "Oh, shit," she muttered. "Stay here, I'll go and get changed."

Jack drove them out of Caerphilly along Mill Road, past Penyrheol and up to the council estate that he had grown up on. They stared at the squat buildings that huddled in the rain, which had eased back to a drizzle: they seeemed to be trying to warm themselves around the meagre light that was given out by the street lamps. Children played in the car parks and streets, ignoring the drizzle, kicking footballs around or chasing each other, their cries and screams high and wild enough to bring goose-flesh to Jack's arms. His mind took him back to his own childhood here, to the winter nights when the alleys that lay between the houses would swallow all light, negating it, wrapping it in a thick cloud of darkness that stifled and suffocated. Sooner or later, the ball he and his friends were playing with would be lost down one of the alleys, and the boys would ritually pick the weakest of their cadre to venture in and find it. Depending on who was playing, Jack had been picked more than once.

In the winter, snow gathered in the alleys, building up in huge drifts, climbing the walls of the houses with searching, ghostly white fingers as if the spectre of some felled giant was attempting to pull himself from the grave. Yet even with the snow, the alleys still seemed to refuse admittance to any but the weakest light thrown by the street lamps, and any ball lost between the houses could take an eternity to find, leaving Jack scrabbling around in the cold gloom. Fear tiptoed behind him, the snow crunching and moving slightly beneath its light footsteps, a sprinkle of powder the only evidence to be seen of its passing when he would spin around to catch a glimpse of it. The ball would always be at the border between the furthest point of grim, pale light and total darkness, so that when he found it he would be face to face with the complete and utter night that lay a mere footstep away and in which he could hear the fear moving gracefully, not bothering to tiptoe now, bold in the absence of light, stepping forward, its tiny, needle-like fingers ready to pierce his heart and hold it steaming before his face, unless he ran, ran now, ran as fast as he could back to his friends and the street lights, back to the real world.

"You okay, Jack?" Rachel looked over at him as he sat shivering.

"Huh? Yeah. Just old memories. Being scared of the dark as a kid, you know?" A moment later he pulled the car over to the side of the road. "Did you bring a torch?" he asked. Rachel held one up, laughing as he breathed a sigh of relief.

"Scared as a kid, eh?" she said, stepping out of the car.

Turning the torch on, they walked down the lane that led to the sty, away from the council estate and into the darkness of the woods.

"There are no cows or anything in this field, are there?" Rachel asked as she climbed over the wooden step, Jack holding the torch and illuminating her footing.

"There weren't yesterday," he said.

"Great," Rachel said, taking the torch from him and returning the favour. "At least we're not going to be found trampled to death." They walked onward, Rachel's walking boots affording her better protection against the mud that Jack slipped in twice, once almost falling on to his backside. The field was open and clear and the early evening moon gave them some light, but they used the torch all the same, working their way across and finally into the tangled undergrowth at its far edge.

"You know, Jack, I'm seriously doubting the wisdom of this."

"You're having a whale of a time, you know you are,"

he said uncertainly, following her through the darkened woods, the beam of light from Rachel's torch occasionally moving from side to side as she lost, then found, the path.

"Just what exactly are we going to do when we get to this pool?" she asked, cursing quietly as a bramble snagged her jeans and tugged at her leg. Jack kept quiet as he walked, trampling down the twigs and branches that tried to trip him up or pull him down into the dead vegetation. The truth was, he had to admit, he had no idea what he was going to do.

"Christ almighty, that's ugly," Rachel said as she stepped out on to the paving stones that surrounded the Dreaming Pool, her torch light flicker over the coral-like surface at the bottom. Jack watched as she picked out nodules and bumps of metallic-coloured rock at random, swinging her beam from one end to another. Around the paving stones, where the man-made met the natural, through the roots and leaves of the trees and plants that grew alongside the pool, a thin, fine mist crawled, seeping into the clearing and caressing the stones before dropping into the empty Pool itself, dissipating in the cool air.

Jack walked around to the other side, opposite Rachel, near the police tape that clicked in the slight wind.
He knelt down at the Pool's edge, looking into the bottom. "Can you bring the torch over here, Rachel?"

"Jack? We have a visitor."

He looked up, then followed Rachel's gaze. The pair of them stared at the head of the path where a young girl stood, surrounded by a faint corona of light. She was perhaps fifteen or sixteen, her close-cropped hair making it difficult to judge her age. She watched them through round, John Lennon glasses, her arms crossed beneath her small breasts. A thin T-shirt covered her chest, cropped short to leave her midriff bare above a pair of cut off denim shorts. On her feet she wore a battered pair of baseball boots.

"*Don't be afraid*," she said, her voice floating across the space between them like a butterfly, quiet and beautiful. "*I'm not here to harm you. I have to speak with you, Jack.*"

"This is fucking weird," he breathed, standing up. The girl smiled at him, unfolding her arms and putting her hands in her pockets. He and Rachel quickly glanced at each other.

The girl looked down at the Pool. "*I used to come swimming here, you know. Much like yourself and Matt.*" She glanced at him. "*Well, Matt anyway. You never heard the story of the Lifeguard, did you?*" Jack dumbly shook his head. "*The Lifeguard was the protector of the Pool. Not just of the children who swam here, but also of the Pool itself. Some said he had been here for years, more than anyone could ever remember, that he had lived forever.*" Her smile disappeared as if falling into the depths of the Pool. "*Trouble is, someone came along and killed him. Your father isn't the only person who has been killed at this place since then, Jack.*"

"Who killed him?"

"*The Lifeguard was killed by agents of the Chapel of the Locus in 1972, four years before you came here that first and only time. Your father was killed by the Chapel also. Your brother has grown up and become one of them. They plan to use this place for a ceremony sometime soon.*"

"Friday," Jack said. "I spoke with my brother today, overheard him talking with another guy. They mentioned some Chapel, this place and Friday."

The girl hung her head at Jack's words, dismayed by his news. She looked over at Rachel, then back at Jack, her glasses catching the faint moonlight. "*The Pool is old, ancient. It has a Spirit of its own which they will try to waken and use, even though they do not understand its nature. Awakening the Pool will only cause them harm. You have to stop them. Somehow, you have to stop them.*"

Jack stepped around the edge of the Pool, his foot steps dull and heavy on the huge stone slabs.

"Excuse me? I don't know who the hell you are and you tell me to get involved in some sort of secret society devil-worshipping thing? You gotta be crazy. Come Wednesday, I'm going to bury --"

"*Cremate,*" the girl said with a smile.

"Very funny. I'm going to cremate my father on Wednesday and that is it. I'm not going to bother with my family ever again if I can help it. Now if you don't mind, we'd like to go home."

The girl looked over at them, her hands still in her pockets, an easy grin on her face as if she knew more than he ever would which, judging by her comments, seemed more than likely to Jack. "*My name is Joanne. Talk to your friend Camilla, Jack. She knows things about the Chapel, about things like this*."

"Camilla?" Jack asked, staring into the dark woods.

"Where'd she go?" Rachel asked, playing the torch light over the area the girl had been standing in a mere second ago. They both walked carefully over to the spot and, turning around, tried to catch sight of her. "Did you know her, Jack?"

"Never saw her before in my life. You think she was a ghost?"

Rachel shone the torch into his eyes, making him throw his hands up in front of his face.

"I don't believe in ghosts, Jack. But normal people do not stand in the woods at night glowing. I don't know what the hell she was."

Jack sighed, running his fingers through his hair. "You want to get out of here?"

"You're damn right I do."

By the time Jack had driven to Newport it was almost nine o'clock. He had dropped Rachel off at her house, promising to call her tomorrow, and once satisfied that she was okay he made his excuses and left. Before driving off he sat in his car, the interior light on, jotting notes in his diary: CHAPEL OF LOCUS (LOCUSTS?) - LIFE-GUARD - JOANNE. Tucking the slim book back into his pocket, he dialled Camilla's number on his mobile, cursing when there was no answer.

Driving back, his mind almost automatically tried to sort the events of the day. His brother had met with the man who had beaten him up in the pub a couple of nights previous, that much was certain. Matt and this other man, Peter, were somehow involved with the Detective Inspector in charge of the case of Jack's father's death which everyone had been told was caused by a wild dog, but which both Matt and (admittedly slightly stranger) his father had claimed was murder. Matt, Peter and the policeman all seemed to be involved in some sort of society called the Chapel, presumably the Chapel of the Locus, and were planning to do something at the Dreaming Pool on Friday.

The thing that Jack found hardest to comprehend was that some of this information had been given to him by what he could only describe as ghosts. That his father was haunting him seemed certain; the girl who had called herself Joanne was something else entirely. Jack had no idea who she was or why she should want to talk with him. In the quiet darkness of the roads between Caerphilly and his home, the thought that he was involved with ghosts, murders and secret societies was baffling enough to Jack. How much more so puzzling would everything sound when he told Camilla about it?

He parked outside his house and with the engine still running, looked at the building. There were no lights on and everything seemed normal...just as it had last night when he returned from the pub. He checked the time and dialled Camilla's number again, counting the rings up to fifteen before giving up. Looking at his house again he dialled Kate, but when she didn't answer he concluded that she must be still at the hospital where she worked as a nurse. Sighing he phoned Gareth and was almost instantly greeted by the voice of his friend's mother.

"Hello, Mrs Miller, it's Jack. Is Gareth there?"

"Oh Jack, hello, yes, one moment, I'll just go and get him. How are you, by the way?" Normally irritated by her habit of talking constantly with whom ever was on the phone, whether the call was for her or her son, Jack now sat back in his seat and gratefully listened to her talk on and on. He was thankful for having a shot of normal lunacy injected into a Sunday which had been beyond belief.

"Jack? Is that you?" Gareth asked, interrupting his mother on the other phone. Mrs Miller spent another few minutes saying goodbye to Jack but eventually hung up. "Sorry about that, man," Gareth said as Jack chuckled.

"No problem, seriously. Listen, can I ask you a favour?"

"Sure, what?"

"Do you mind if I crash at your place tonight?"

"My place?" "If that's okay, I mean, I don't want to cause any hassle or anything."

"No, no, it's no problem," Gareth said. "How come, though?"

Jack sighed "You really don't want to know, mate. It'll only be for one night, though."

"That's okay, it's just . . . I don't know, it's just a bit weird, you asking to stay at my place. It's usually the other way around."

"Yeah, I know. Listen, I'll get some gear from my place and come over, okay? I should only be about half an hour or so, and I think your mum's run up a big enough bill on my mobile already."

"Your fault, mate. You know what she's like."

Jack laughed and said goodbye to his friend, then looked across at his house.

The living room light had been switched on.

"Oh shit," he whispered. He made up his mind that he could manage without clean clothes for one night, and drove over to Gareth's house.

4: MONDAY

Jack spent most of Monday morning over at his friend's house, tucked away in his bedroom which, like Gareth, was still stuck in the long-haired heavy-metal phase of their teenage years. The walls were dotted with mostly old posters of various rock bands, with a liberal sprinkling of concert tickets that Gareth had kept as souvenirs.

On the inside of his door hung last year's Page Three calendar, a topless blonde girl smiling out at the pair of them. Gareth's stereo, still plastered with stickers of band logos from yesteryear, had played almost exactly the same music for the last ten years, its tired needle digging new grooves in old records.

"This is the best Maiden album," Gareth said. taking a record out of his large collection. *Number of The Beast* might have had more commercial success, but *Killers* is when they were at their peak. The best line-up and the best songs." Jack watched, smirking despite himself as his friend almost reverentially placed the vinyl onto his turntable, lifting the arm over and on to the record.
The speakers coughed up a burst of crackling and static as the needle connected, and Gareth turned the volume down as the intro started up.

"Why don't you buy a new needle, Gar? That thing sounds ancient."

"I keep meaning to," he said, tapping out the drum beat on his thighs, "but I just never get around to it. I kinda like the way old vinyl sounds with an old needle, anyway."

Jack shook his head in resignation and lit up a cigarette, throwing one over to Gareth. Using a nearby take away curry container as an ashtray the pair sat through the instrumental that started Iron Maiden's second album. As the second song began, Gareth asked,

"How come you didn't want to stay at your place last night?"

Jack shrugged. "Long story, mate."

"I ain't going anywhere." Gareth was unemployed again. Jack had lost count of the number of jobs both temporary and permanent, his friend had had, since they left school; through various circumstances Gareth had lost them all. Most of his jobs had ended through no fault of his own; three of the firms he had worked for had all gone bust within the first few months of Gareth's employment. Jack had almost offered him a job in the shop where he had worked, but had reconsidered. He was not one to believe in jinxes or people who were bad luck, but neither was he about to tempt fate. He thought of telling Gareth everything, about his father's death and his brother's possible involvement, about the Dreaming Pool and Rachel, about the ghosts of his father and the girl called Joanne, but waved it all away as if it meant nothing.

"Was it to do with that bloke who hit you in the pub the other night?" Gareth asked.

"Kind of." Before he could stop himself, Jack was telling his friend a small pack of lies, inventing a scenario in which he had glimpsed the attacker waiting for him near his home the previous night and so had thought better of going there.

"Jesus. You ought to get the cops in."

Jack said he was thinking about it. A little uncomfortable with his lies, as well as the second-hand chair he was sitting in, he made his excuses and got up to go. "Do you want me to come back with you?" Gareth offered.

"No, I should be okay, mate. Don't worry. You going up the pub tonight?"

"Nah, I'm skint. My giro doesn't come through till Thursday."

"I'll get you a couple, pay you back for putting me up here."

Gareth shrugged. "Maybe. Do you know if Camilla or Annie are going to be out?"

With a supreme effort of will, Jack stopped himself from smiling. "I'm not sure. I'll give you a ring later, okay? Say ta-ra to your mum for me, all right?"

On the short drive back to his own place, Jack couldn't stop chuckling at his friend's obvious optimism concerning women. A couple of days ago he had been desperate to ask out the girl Jack had picked up at the party (why couldn't he remember her name for more than five minutes?) and now he was basing his decisions about going out on whether or not Camilla, or more importantly her friend Annie, were going to be there, despite the fact, Jack was sure, that he would run screaming in the opposite direction if she made any move toward him.

Unlocking the door to his house, Jack was instantly assailed by the scent of mixed herbs and spices. With no small amount of trepidation he put his head round the door and looked at the mess that had been made of his kitchen. Although he found it somewhat difficult in the light of day to blame a ghost, it was some comfort to know that he hadn't hallucinated the episode. Before heading upstairs to shower and change, he phoned Camilla.

"And where were you last night?" he asked when she picked up.

"Never you mind," she said with a laugh. They chatted for a moment or two, Jack playfully trying to find out if she had a new boyfriend before asking her if the Chapel of the Locus meant anything to her. "It rings vague bells. Why's that?"

"You'd be a complete angel if you'd have a hunt around in your books and find out anything about it. It's probably Locus, L-O-C-U-S, but it might be Locusts as in big grasshoppers. I'd be eternally grateful to you, my dear."

"Of course you would, Jack. Like I say, it sounds familiar."

"Any chance I could pop round this afternoon and see what you've got?"

"You are keen, aren't you? Why the rush?"

"Let's just say personal reasons, shall we?"

"Ooh, Jack Bradley, man of mystery, all of a sudden. All right, what time do you want to come round?"

Jack looked at his watch. "I've gotta go into town first and get a couple of things . . . say about half four, five?"

"Yeah, that'll be fine. See you then."

Jack put the phone down and turned to look at the kitchen door. Not yet ready to face the herbal chaos of the room, he picked up the phone again and dialled the office where, on a normal day, he would already have been at work. His boss was understanding, telling him to take a week or two of compassionate leave when Jack told her about his father's death.

"Come in when you're ready, Jack. Let me know and we'll sort out leave and whatever then, okay?"

"Yeah, okay. Cheers, Joyce." He hung up and, after a moment's hesitation, forced himself to open the door to the kitchen and survey the mess seriously. Before he went into town, he thought, he was going to have to tidy this place up.

As he walked through the pedestrianised centre of Newport some time later, his hair still drying from the shower he had taken to rid himself of the pungent odours of various spices and cleaning products, Jack found himself wondering whether or not he was going insane. Since Friday, his life had turned upside down-- he was related to a possible murderer, ghosts and spirits were visiting him and he was terrified of spending a night in his own house-- yet here he was, shopping for a suit to wear to his father's funeral in a couple of days as if nothing had changed. Something in the world was not right, he reasoned, stepping into Burton's. A half hour later, he left the shop with a black suit that may as well have had FOR JOB INTERVIEWS AND FUNERALS ONLY written all over it.

While he had waited for Rachel yesterday, he'd thought about the funeral he had witnessed and how the world continued on regardless of anyone's death. Walking back to his car with his new suit neatly folded in a carrier bag, he wondered whether his father would share his views. Jack had never been religious -- church and God were just things he had studied in school-- but it was still a shock to realise that he had seen proof of some sort of afterlife, even if it was not the traditional pearly gates and cherubs of the Christian world. Somehow his father had remained in the real world, refusing to go on to . . . well, to whatever lay beyond, if anything. Was that because he had been murdered and, in the way of all ghosts (if Hollywood was to be believed), he couldn't "move on" until his soul was finally laid to rest, or his murderer brought to justice? Was that why he had charged Jack with discovering the name of his killer?

"You're thinking like a lunatic, Jack," he told himself when he reached his car, opened the boot and bundled in his suit. Sitting in the driver's seat and lighting up a cigarette, he stared out at the dark car park. The weak fluorescent tubes did little except hint at light, casting much of the place into shadow. People moved to and from their vehicles, going about their everyday business of shopping and living, trailing their families through the ocean of dirt and darkness, touching only briefly the small pools of half-light before plunging once again into the unknown waters of gloom.

Rubbing at his eyes, Jack was surprised to feel a tear or two there. For the first time he realised that he actually missed his father and had missed him for the last seven years. Brushing his tears away, Jack decided to stay at his house that evening and wait for his father's ghost to visit him.

"So what you got for me?"Jack asked Camilla later that afternoon, sitting down in one of the plush chairs in her living room. Camilla's parents were wealthy, to say the least, and when she had turned eighteen had bought her her own house to teach her to stand on her own two feet. Paying for the house outright and for the small amount of renovation the place had needed, not to mention the furnishings and carpets did not seem to Jack to be the best way to start their daughter off on the road to independence. The monthly allowance paid to her from a trust fund set up by her parents allowed her to do pretty much what she wanted however giving her plenty of time to delve into the world of conspiracy theories, secret societies and the like.

She sat on the floor in front of him, three large books opened at various pages before her, a cup of herbal tea at her side.

"Not a great deal, I'm afraid. Your Chapel of the Locus is practically unknown." She cleared her throat, placed the first book on her lap and skimmed down the page. "In May 1776, a former Jesuit priest named Adam Weishaupt founded a secret society within the already established Masonic

Lodges in Germany, so that he had a secret society hidden within a secret society. He was, of course, already a Freemason and only allowed other Freemasons to join him. They were rationalists and republicans, intent on establishing their own world order through just about any means and were officially suppressed by the Bavarian government only nine years later in 1785, although in actual fact they merely went underground and continue to this day in positions of almost supreme power."

"And they're the Chapel of the Locus?" Jack asked.

"No, of course not. Weishaupt created the Illuminati!" Camilla said as if everyone should know that.

Jack sighed. "They're the guys who're going to be at the Egyptian pyramids at the turn of the century, right?"

"Mock all you like, Jack. The facts I've just given you can be confirmed just about anywhere. There's a whole lot more about the Illuminati that most people wouldn't believe, like Weishaupt impersonating George Washington." Camilla raised an eyebrow at him, daring him to question her.

"And the Chapel?" Jack asked. The last thing he wanted was to get into another conversation with Camilla about how the Illuminati were ruling the world. She pouted a little, disappointed he hadn't taken the bait, then put the first book down and picked up another.

"Weishaupt died in 1830, according to the history books a broken man, but then history is always written by the victorious. Two pupils and close friends of his, Josef Durer and Gustav von Juntz, were with him in the years leading up to his death and were at his bedside when he died. Weishaupt charged them, two of the greatest of his Illuminati, with continuing his own secret work which he had kept hidden from the other members. They travelled to England and nothing more was heard of them until . . ."

Camilla swapped books, picking up the last of her references. She ran her finger down the page until she found what she was looking for. "Until, in 1836, Josef Durer is mentioned briefly as a visitor to the court of the then princess Victoria and not the king, William IV, using the title of 'Bishop of the Chapel'. He was given lands by her in 'the West

Country and the Marches' where, it says here somewhat melodramatically, 'he and his fellows pursued their dreams'." She snapped the book shut. "And that's it."

"That's it?" Jack asked.

"Apart from the fact that Victoria became Queen the very next year, which makes you wonder, eh?" She shrugged. "Sorry, but I can't find anything else, and nowhere I've looked has there been a specific mention of a Chapel of the Locus. Or Locusts," she added with a chuckle.

"Not much, is it?" He sat back in his chair and finished off the remains of his tea. "Do you know what a Locus is?"

Camilla stood up, wincing as her knee joints popped loudly, and hobbled over to her bookcase where she pulled out her dictionary. "It's Latin," she said when she found it, "meaning place. Plural is loci, L-O-C-I, not the Norse god. A position or point, especially in a text or treatise. Or, in maths, a curve formed by satisfying all the points in a given equation or a whole host of other things to do with lines and points and surfaces." She closed the book and put it back on the shelf. "I think we both know what a locust is."

"Bugger," he said softly. "I was kind of hoping you could tell me just about everything. Ah well. You going up the pub tonight?" He smiled knowingly. "Gareth was asking me earlier."

"No, I've got to visit my parents. I think Kate said she was going up, though, if you want to give her a ring." She returned his smile."

"Annie said she'd be interested in a beer tonight . . . but only if Gareth was going."

"You're joking?"

Camilla shook her head. "Nope, she thought he was great. Didn't care what others thought of how he looked, spoke his mind, that sort of thing. Seems to have caught her interest."

"God, a girl actually interested in him as opposed to the other way round. What the hell's he going to do?"

"Who knows? If he is going out, give me a ring and I'll let Annie know."

"Yeah, I will do." He paused, thinking back to what Camilla had found out. "Pursued their dreams?' What do you think that means?"

"Could be anything," she said. "As an offshoot of the Illuminati, their dreams would probably have been of world domination." Jack looked at her quizzically. "What?" she asked.

"Nothing. Just do me a favour, eh? Don't ever go changing." With that Jack said his farewells and drove home.

When he got in, he phoned Kate who said that she wouldn't be at the pub, then phoned Gareth to tell him that neither of the girls would be out that evening but that Annie fancied a drink if he was interested. He smiled at the stunned silence that followed until Gareth said,

"No, I can't, I'm skint like I said."

"Well, I said I'd get you a couple."

"No, it's okay, mate. Give me a ring tomorrow if you like."

"What, are you going to be less skint then?" Jack asked with a laugh. "I thought you said your dole didn't come until Thursday?" Gareth made various embarrassed noises, muttering vaguely about wanting to work on something that evening. Listening to him, Jack couldn't help but smile at his poor excuses. "All right, I'll call you tomorrow or Wednesday, how's that?"

"Yeah, fine. No problem."

Jack spent the rest of that evening tidying his house, putting away the various paperbacks that he had started to read and then forgotten about, many with bookmarks made out of scraps of paper still inside them. He put something mellow on the stereo, humming along as he washed and wiped the few dirty dishes he had left around the place, before running the vacuum cleaner over the place and dusting the frame of his Gustav Doré, print. He even went so far as to empty out the ashtrays that had inevitably accumlated in each of his rooms, all of them brimming over with ash and butts. Every time he emptied them, which admittedly wasn't that often, he always shook his head and thought that even if he didn't quit outright, he'd still have to cut down.
By the time he was shaking the ash from the last one into the bin, another cigarette hung smoking from his lips.

He made himself something to eat and sat down in front of the TV. Only as he skimmed through the channels did he realise that he had tidied his entire house as if expecting a visitor. His supper was left to go cold when he remembered who that visitor was.

Footsteps woke him. A late-night film ran strobe lights across his eyes as he sat up on the sofa, jarred back into the world of the conscious by the sound of some huge being walking slowly down the stairs. He glanced quickly at the door to the living room: it was closed. Pushing his supper plate off to one side, Jack stood up and turned the light on, then the TV off and stared at the plain white door as his father approached it from the other side.

Darkness seeped in around the doorjamb, sliding in through the small gap, negating the light, creeping in through the cracks around the panels in the door, the wood groaning as something pushed against it from outside.

"**Jack**."

He almost answered. He had been resigned to this meeting all day. He had even made an effort to prepare his house for this moment. Yet now he hesitated. The voice that said his name was deep and rich, full of confidence and malice, so different from the plaintive querying of his father's first appearance. It hadn't been a question, and it hadn't been his father's voice.

"**Answer me, Jack.**"

Whatever was beyond that door, Jack was certain, it wasn't the ghost of his father. He looked around the room, knowing that the only other exit was the front window, and turned back when the door gave out another groan, the wood stretching impossibly as a hand was pressed into it, the centre of the door bulging inwards, a hand print clearly visible.

"Who are you?" Jack called, feeling his legs begin to shake. The hand in the door was pulled back, the wood slowly, achingly settling back into place. There was silence. Jack stood in the middle of his living room, unable to take his gaze from the door, his whole body straining for some sound or sign that whoever was behind the door had either left or was still there, anything to let him know one way or the other, to end the uncertainty, to allow him to react to something instead of this hanging in time, poised like a fish about to bite on a hooked worm, still in the water, yet with the possibility of being dragged thrashing into the air.

The door exploded and darkness filled the room.

Jack yelled, throwing his hands up in front of his face as he was peppered with tiny pieces of wood, feeling splinters and larger shards punch into his flesh as he fell backwards and crashed on to the floor.

He blinked several times in the utter darkness, unsure whether he was unconscious or blind. Gingerly he ran his hand across his forehead, wincing as he dislodged or embedded pieces of his door, and felt small trickles of blood dribbling down his face; then the sharp beestings from what seemed to be a million other similar injuries suddenly rushed upwards to flood his brain with a swollen river of pain.

"Fuck!" he cried, rolling to either side with his arms around his body, crying out as he inadvertently pushed more splinters, tiny daggers of wood, into himself.

"**Jack**." The voice was right next to him, practically breathing into his ear. He rolled away from it and came up against the tiled fireplace, banging his head sharply on one of the corners, swearing again. "**You should have answered me, Jack**."

He was lifted suddenly, hands grabbing his upper arms, pinning them to his body and lifting him up, his feet leaving the floor and dangling uselessly in the blackness. He sobbed as yet more wood was pressed into his skin, coupled with the pain caused by his assailant's fingers that gripped like vises, threatening to turn his bones to powder while his eyes streamed tears that did nothing to wash away the impenetrable cloud of darkness that enveloped the pair of them.

"Who are you?" he gasped.

"**I missed you last night, Jack**," the voice said, the words carried on a gust of fetid breath that almost made him gag. "**We could have done all this last night in a much more pleasant manner**." He was flung through the air, the thing turning and letting go of him all at once, sending him through the darkness to crash on to the sofa. **"I dislike unnecessary displays of force. I find them vulgar and demeaning**."

Jack flinched from the breath that was once again in his face. He hadn't heard the thing move, but it was instantly in his face as if it were omnipresent, not so much *in* the darkness as *of* it, permeating its substance, able to be anywhere within it at all times like a god in the void.

"What . . . what do you want?" Jack managed.
He drew his legs up on to the sofa, heedless of the pain this movement caused, and wrapped his aching, bloodied arms around his knees, pulling himself up into a ball.

"Who killed me, Jack? Who killed your father?"

"You're not my father." All around him, the darkness, the negativity chuckled, the sound of a bottomless throat rattling vocal chords made of chains.

"I'm hurt, Jack." Something stroked the top of his head, parting his hair like a handful of worms trailing through his scalp, making him moan and shiver. **"Who killed me, Jack?"**

"Oh Christ help me," Jack cried, feeling his tears mixing with the blood that was drying on his face.

"Who killed me, Jack?"

The worms on his head separated, sliding over his skin, searching out his ears, wriggling and squirming, writhing over one another in their haste to penetrate his skull. He screamed, covering his ears with his hands, feeling the thin tendrils move beneath his palms.

"The Chapel of the Locus! The Chapel of the Locus!", screamed Jack. The thing sighed, a deep roll of satisfaction, and Jack felt it pull back as if standing, the worms lifting from him. As he keeled over and lay sobbing on the sofa, the darkness slipped quietly from the room and the walls and furnishings were revealed as if a shadow were being chased away by the rising sun, though there was only the stark illumination of a light bulb above him as he cried and bled.

"I'm sorry I couldn't stop that, Jack."

"Joanne?" Jack looked down at the young girl, still wearing her T-shirt, shorts and glasses. She sat on the side of a hill overlooking a sprawling town in the warmth of the midday sun.

"Where am I?"

"You're on your sofa at home. It might be a good idea to phone an ambulance when you wake up in the morning."

"Wake up? I'm dreaming?"

Joanne held her hand up and waggled it from side to side.

"Sort of." Jack looked around. The hill was perfectly smooth from its base to its rounded top, and the town that lay below them stretched away in perfectly ordered squares to the horizon where it met the perfectly blue sky. He turned back to her, indicating the view.

"So I dreamt all this up to get away from . . . from what happened?"

She shook her head, patting the ground next to her, indicating he should sit. *"No. I brought you here. This is kind of where I live."*

He sat down next to her and they were silent for a moment, relaxing in the moderate heat of an unseen sun.

"Who are you?" he asked, feeling that he'd asked that question a few too many times that evening.

"My name's Joanne, but you know that already. As to who I am . . . I suppose you mean who was I?" She pulled her legs up and rested her arms on them, placing her chin on them in turn, pushing her John Lennon glasses further up her nose with one finger.

"My name's Joanne Daniels. I was born in Cardiff in 1958 and when I was sixteen, I was ritually murdered by the Chapel of the Locus at the Dreaming Pool." She glanced over at him, smiling sadly. *"Not much of a story, eh?"*

"So . . . you're a ghost?" Jack asked softly. Sitting here, on the borderlands of this dream world, she seemed real enough to him.

Joanne gazed off into the distance. *"I don't know, Jack. I'm not sure if this is heaven, though it's pleasant enough. I can't leave here, except to visit the area around the Dreaming Pool, though I can bring people to this place through their dreams. Over twenty years have drifted by since I was killed. The last thing I remember of my real life . . . well, I don't want to remember the last thing I remember.*" She sighed, changing the subject. "*I saw your father murdered, Jack, and wanted to stop it somehow but I couldn't. When you visited the Pool, I knew I should try and talk to you, but I couldn't do that either.*"

"But you did. You spoke to me when me and Rachel went up there," Jack said, but she shook her head again.

"*No, that was the second time you visited. The first time I couldn't show myself because of . . .*" She trailed off, scratching idly at her arm as if for want of something to do.

"Because of my brother?" Jack asked. "Would he have seen you too?" Joanne nodded. "Why didn't you want him to -- " He stopped as realisation dawned upon him. "Did Matt kill you? Did he do it?"

"*No, he was far too young then. He didn't even know the Chapel existed.*" She looked at him again, reached out and held his hand. "*Your friend Camilla is half right. They want to rule, maybe not the world, but as much as they can. They're small and petty-minded, like every other group of bad guys in a book or a movie.*" She turned to him and looked at him earnestly, impressing the importance of her words on him. "*But they want to bring something into the world which isn't small, which isn't just another monster from Hell. They're trying to conjure something which doesn't understand them or their ambitions. They want to control it but they don't realise that they can't and that it's going to get loose.*"

"And is that what . . . what visited me this evening?"

"*That was a small part of it, the Voice. Jack, I don't know what they intend to do with it, but when they find out that they can't control it...*" She paused. "*They have to be stopped and you have to do it. You have to find the Lifeguard.*"

Jack laughed and shook his head. "The Lifeguard? Joanne, you have been watching far too many bad movies. There's a secret cult that wants to raise up some sort of demon and I have to stop them by finding some guy called the Lifeguard? I'm guessing that this creature will appear on

Friday at the Dreaming Pool?" Joanne nodded intently, making Jack laugh again. "You sound like a boxing promoter: Live at the Dreaming Pool this Friday, Jack Bradley struggles to take the WBA heavyweight title from Beelzebub the Pit Monster!" His voice boomed out into the quiet world.

"*You can still mock me after what happened to you this evening?*" Jack slipped his arm around her thin shoulders, pulling her to his side where her head rested on his shoulder.

"You're thinking in black and white, Jo. Good and evil, right and wrong, we're the good guys, they're the bad guys. What about the grey areas in between?"

"*What do you mean?*"

"Well, what's stopping them controlling this bog monster?"

"*Your brother, Matt. He thinks he can keep the Spirit under his control, but he won't be able to.*"

"Why not?"

"*He doesn't realise that he's . . . he's not eligible.*"

Jack paused, trying to get his thoughts in order, stroking her arm as if to warm her though the midday sun drove out any chills.

"It can't just be me and you against the Chapel and their pet demon, can it? Surely someone else knows about them, someone more...I don't know...qualified to go up against them? This Lifeguard, for example. The old one's dead so I have to find a new one, right? Where do I look?"

"*No, it is the Spirit of the Lifeguard you have to find. His body's dead, but he can be revived,*" she said quickly as Jack groaned. "*The Chapel killed him two years before me and locked his essence away. You have to find it.*"

"Why me?"

Joanne raised her head and looked up at him, her white teeth shining as she smiled.

"*Who on earth could be more qualified than someone who's lost his father to the Chapel, and his brother in a different way, and who's been haunted by the thing they want to bring into the world?*"

"You're still thinking in black and white, Jo,"

he said. They stared at each other until Jo lifted her head, eyes half closed, lips half open. For a second Jack found himself responding, pulling her closer but then he blinked and drew back suddenly.

"*What's wrong?*" she asked. Jack shook his head.

"I can't, Jo. Sorry."

She stood up and stepped away from him. "*It's because of what I am, isn't it? Because I'm . . . I'm a ghost.*"

"No," he said quickly. He sighed and looked out over the neatly structured town, the houses arranged like the squares of a chess board. "No," Jack repeated softly. "If anything it's because of Rachel." Jo turned to him. " I think . . . I don't know. I think we might have something going."

"*Sorry,*" Jo said quietly after a moment. "*I thought you . . . that we could have . . .*" Her words trailed off. "*Perhaps you should leave,*"

Jack nodded and stood, having no idea of how to get out of this place. "*Best of luck, Jack,*" Jo said. Jack started to say something but yawned instead. A second ago he had been wide awake, but now . . .

He slept.

5: TUESDAY

"I hate to keep saying this Jack, but you look like shit."

He and Rachel sat in a cafe called Scarlett's, drinking tea and chatting. She called him at lunch time as she had taken the day off, wondering if they were ever going to get out together. Jack had spent most of the morning in the casualty department of the Royal Gwent Hospital having a large number of splinters and wood fragments pulled out of various parts of his body. The larger cuts had been covered with sticking plasters and, on his upper arms at least, with bandages as well. His face looked as if he had either had a recent case of chickenpox or had broken out in teenage acne again, as small, dark red scabs were scattered across his still-bruised nose, cheeks and forehead like badly concealed mines in a field. Rachel, on the other hand, looked as fresh and bright as ever, her long dark hair undone and rolling in strong curls most of the way down her back. Looking at her sitting opposite him wearing jeans and a sweatshirt, Jack realised just how good-looking she was.

"I wish I could say the same about you," he said, "but I can't."

"Why, Mr Bradley. Are you flirting with me?" She grinned, dimples appearing on her cheeks; Jack smiled in return, wincing at his still tender wounds. "I sent my boyfriend packing yesterday," she said suddenly, staring into her mug of tea as she did so. Jack stayed silent. "Don't worry, that's not a pressure thing." She looked up at him, smiling again. "We'd just about run out of reasons to stay together anyway, so I would've dumped him even if I hadn't taken a shine to you."

"Is that what you've done?"

"Well, I don't normally get irritated by blokes who say they're going to phone me and then don't, unless I happen to like them." Rachel watched as Jack almost blushed in front of her, grinning despite himself. "But on a more serious note, what have you done about that Pool and your brother and everything?"

Jack sighed and wished he'd brought his cigarettes with him but, as a concession to Rachel, he'd deliberately left them at home. He started to bite on nails instead.

"I spoke with a friend of mine yesterday and she gave me a little bit of background on the Chapel of the Locus, but not a great deal. I haven't seen or heard from Matt since Sunday." He sighed, staring out the window at the high street as the few people who had ventured out into the drizzle scurried along-- older women carrying shopping, young mothers either pushing prams or pulling children, groups of kids not old enough to be out of school smoking cigarettes brazenly. "I should phone my mother as well, find out what's happening tomorrow."

"The funeral's at three o'clock. Best to get to the crematorium by about half two," Rachel said automatically. After a pause she said, "For what it's worth, the local paper in Caerphilly had a bit about your father's death in it last night." Jack raised an eyebrow at her, sipping at his tea. "Apparently, according to the police, he was savaged by a wild dog, which has now been caught and put down. End of story. End of case."

Jack sat back in his chair and stared at her, wondering what it would feel like to run his fingers through her hair, before Rachel snapped her fingers in front of him. "Concentrate, Jack," she said.

"I don't know what to do, Rache," he said sadly. He took a deep breath. "I had a dream last night, after everything happened." He had told Rachel earlier about his "visitor" and the damage that had been done to his house and his own person. "I saw the girl from the Pool, Joanne. She said the Chapel were planning to raise some sort of demon at the Pool on Friday, and that I had to stop it."

"Seriously?" Rachel said with a straight face. Jack nodded. The silence stretched for perhaps a minute before the pair of them burst into laughter, the other customers around them glancing over their shoulders to look at the noisy couple near the window. "So let's get this straight: last night you were visited and terrorised by some sort of force or ghost or something that beat you up and blew down your living room door -- "

"He huffed and he puffed and he blew the door in," Jack interrupted with a smile.

"Whatever. He wrecks your door and leaves you all beaten up, then you dream of another ghost who tells you to stop a secret society from raising some sort of demon?"

"That's about it," Jack said, glad to be laughing about it. That morning, lying on a bed in the casualty department of the hospital and having splinters pulled out of him by some latter-day Inquisition torturer, the had half wondered about his sanity because the whole thing had seemed so real. He even considered telling the nurse about the whole episode.

Rachel looked at him, her smile gone. "Jack, if that stuff hadn't happened at the Pool on Sunday night, I think I would have walked out of here by now." She pushed her mug over to the side, reached across the table and took hold of his hands, looking into his eyes and lowering her voice. "I don't know exactly what happened that night, but I saw that girl Joanne. She existed, and I heard every word she said to you. I'm not a Christian, I don't believe in God and I don't believe in the Devil. I've never seen a UFO or met an alien and I don't believe in ghosts, but what happened on Sunday scared me, Jack, more than I let on. I spent the whole of yesterday thinking about it. Joanne exists and I think you should take her seriously."

Rachel let go of his hands and sat back.

"Sorry if I've spoilt the mood."

Jack shook his head. "I just don't know what to do, Rache," he said finally. "All of a sudden, I've been elected ghostbuster and I don't know what to do."

"Let's have another cuppa," Rachel said, digging into her pockets for her money, "and then we'll visit the library."

"The library?"

"Why not? If nothing else, they might actually have something on the Dreaming Pool. Something as ugly as that thing is can't have been ignored for years.

If you're right and kids have been swimming there for ages, or used to swim anyway, then surely someone would have written something about it?"

Newport Reference Library was exactly the same as every other library in the world: stuffed full of books with far too few assistants, and almost quintessentially quiet. Rachel managed to track down someone who was actually working there and, after receiving a dark look, (as if they had no right to disturb the assistant's work and ought to be ashamed of themselves,) they were directed to the history section. They smiled at each other, amused yet almost scared to talk about the woman in case she suddenly popped out from between the books like some predatory librarian in a cartoon, finger to her lips, eyes wide as she "sshhhhhed" them.

Taking two books each, all dealing with Caerphilly and its surrounding area at the start of the nineteenth century, they sat down and started going through them. Rachel placed a pen and notepad between them for notes.

Almost an hour later, the notepad sat there as new and empty as when Rachel had bought it. Rubbing at his eyes, wincing as he accidentally poked one of his scabs, Jack sat back, pushing the heavy book off his lap and onto the desk. Looking over at her, he picked up the pen and pad and wrote THIS IS HOPELESS. She smiled and nodded at him, turning back to her book.

Jack looked around the place, smiling slightly at the one or two people who caught his eye briefly before they returned to their books. He noted how many of them were students, or at least appeared to be: most with their hair either straight and long or in dreadlocks, with canvas bags stuffed full of files and note books, busy studying for exams or tests or something. Jack normally felt proud that he'd never been a student; he'd finished comprehensive school at sixteen and had run straight out to meet the real world, refusing to be hidden within the safe world of education for a moment longer. Now he wondered whether he would have ended up with better jobs if he'd stayed at school or gone on to university, or if he was just being naive.

Rachel tapped him on the shoulder and pointed to a passage in the book she was now thrusting in front of him. As she leaned next to him, Jack read:

In records of the church meetings in 1839, mention is made of the payment of £7.13s.4d. to John Sharpe for the rent of the Old Barn to a Father Durér and "his small band of priests" who remained in Caerphilly throughout the winter. Conn Usher is recorded, the following summer, as receiving 16s.8d. for the straw used in thatching the wooden chapel built for Father Durer in 1840, a few miles outside of Caerphilly. Capel Pwynt (translated as Chapel Point) was completed on the sight of a pagan worshipping ground and the five monks who lived within its confines deliberately built their retreat there to discourage any continuance of what Father Durér wrote of as being 'the most vile practices to ancient devils'. The focus of the worship was an old pool, naturally formed yet surrounded by huge slabs of cut and shaped stone, each etched with scenes describing the sacrifices that were said to take place there.

"Jesus," Jack whispered.

"That's it, isn't it?" Rachel asked. Jack nodded.

"According to Camilla, Father Josef Durer was the member of the Chapel that apparently bought or got the land from Queen Victoria around 1830. He and his mates obviously built their own little church up there, pretending to be Christians. Locus is Latin for 'points' or 'positions'. Chapel Point is the Chapel of the Locus, and the pool that they mention is obviously the Dreaming Pool."

"What about the stones? The book says they're etched with designs. I didn't see any on Sunday."

"Maybe they've worn off, been eroded or something."

Jack fell silent, running his hand through his hair, desperate for a cigarette to help him think. "This doesn't really say anything, does it?" he said softly. "I mean, all it says is that Camilla was right about the Chapel of the Locus getting some land in Wales, and that it was up around the Dreaming Pool. It doesn't say anything about what's going to happen on Friday or how we can stop it."

A scrap of paper, rolled up into a ball, suddenly landed on the desk in front of them.
They stared at it until Rachel picked it up, then looked around the room. Everyone else was busy with their books. No one was looking at them.

"What does it say?" Jack asked. Rachel unrolled it, smoothing it on the book. In small letters, the message SHUT THE FUCK UP! was neatly printed across it. She crumpled it back up and looked around again, this time catching the eye of a girl with a shaven head and nose rings who scowled at her until Rachel dropped her gaze.

"Shall we get going?" she said.

They left the library, bought some chips and sat in John Frost Square on one of the cold and slightly damp benches surrounding a sparsely leafed tree. There they threw some chips to the pigeons that instantly gathered around them. The large clock that dominated the square showed half past four, the strange halfway point just after most shoppers had left the town centre for their homes, but before the majority of workers either filtered out of their offices or poured from the buses that stopped at the station connected to one corner of the square. Jack had offered to take Rachel back up to his house but she had turned him down, settling for a seat in the fresh, if somewhat chilly, air instead.

"You said you haven't seen Matt since Sunday?" she asked. Jack held a chip out to a pigeon brave enough to stand on the bench beside him, and watched as it pecked repeatedly at the greasy food.

"Nope. Christ knows what I'm going to--ow!" He pulled his hand back quickly, startling the pigeon that had tried to take off his finger with the remains of the chip. Rachel laughed at him, pointing as the pigeon, oblivious to its mistake, fluttered around for a second before landing back on the bench looking for more food. "Little bastard," Jack muttered, glaring at the bird. He tossed another chip at it, smiling slightly as it hit the pigeon in the head before falling to the ground where one of the bird's many comrades quickly ate it.

"Oh, you're so tough, Mr Bradley," Rachel said, cuddling up to him and fluttering her eyelashes.

"And you're too sarcastic for your own good," Jack said, leaning down suddenly and kissing her briefly.

"That all I'm going to get?" Rachel asked. And with that they held each other and kissed, unmindful of the few stares they received from the last of the days' shoppers as they kissed, surrounded by the pigeons feasting on and squabbling over their forgotten chips.

"You're more than welcome to stay the night at my place, you know," said Jack. They were walking up Stow Hill hand in hand, heading past the cathedral towards Jack's house. Rachel had travelled down on the train with the understanding that they would probably go to a pub for lunch, but Scarlett's had won out so Jack had offered to drive her home.

"Is that so you could leap on me and take advantage of me?" she asked him.

"Maybe." He smiled at her.

"Or is it because you don't want to be alone with that . . . thing again?"

Jack sighed. "Yeah, that's partly it. Sure I can't tempt you with a cup of tea at least?" he said, indicating his house on the left as they drew level with it. Rachel looked it over, noting the large but slightly unkempt lawn with its overflowing rubbish bins on one side, and the long drive where Jack's car sat.

"Not bad," she said with more than a hint of sarcasm. "But I've got work tomorrow, remember?"

Reluctant to let her leave, but unable to stop her, Jack unlocked the passenger door for her, and climbed into the driver's seat once she was in. As they headed out of Newport and towards Caerphilly, Rachel asked him what it was that he did.

"How do you mean?"

"Well, you said the other day that you don't really know what your brother does for a living. I was wondering if this is something that runs in the Bradley family, because I don't know what you do."

Jack smiled and glanced over at her. "Before I tell you, you have to tell me truthfully whether or not you like me."

Rachel frowned. "I only get an answer if I massage your ego first?" Jack nodded, grinning. "As a matter of fact, Bradley, I'm not in the habit of going out to meet guys whom I hardly know just because I've got nothing else to do. Even if Sunday hadn't happened, I think I would have found an excuse to come and see you today. Good enough?"

"Oh, I think it'll do," he said, then fell silent.

"Well? What do you do?"

"As little as possible," He chuckled at Rachel's exasperated expression. "Truthfully, I happen to be one of the government's slaves, toiling away for an absolute pittance." He glanced at her, noting her crossed arms and pursed lips. With a sweep of his arm, his voice laden with sarcasm, Jack proclaimed "I . . . am a civil servant!"

"A civil servant? Where?"

Jack's grin widened as he kept her waiting. "Don't make me ask you again, Bradley," Rachel said raising a fist as he laughed.

"The National Office of Statistics. I deal with very sad and boring people who want to know how many pints of milk the average corner shop sells. Not very glamorous, eh?"

"Is it any better than working with the dead?"

"Is there much difference?" Jack laughed.

They fell silent, watching the scenery change from the busy outskirts of Newport to the long winding road which was little more than a lane in some places. The hills on either side of the road started to creep upwards and the fields became larger as they moved into farmland, and dusk settled over everything as if tucking the world up, getting it ready for bed.

"You know, Rache, we don't actually know much about this thing that's happening on Friday. I mean, sure, we know the Chapel of the Locus existed back in the 1830s and that they built some sort of church up by the Dreaming Pool, but we don't know anything that's going to help prevent them from raising up the devil or whatever." He flicked the windscreen wipers on as it began to rain gently.

"What about Joanne?" Jack looked over at her. "The girl from the Pool? The ghost? Maybe she knows something."

"Maybe," Jack said quietly, thinking back to the night before and feeling guilty for almost having kissed her.

"Why don't we go up to the Pool when we get to Caerphilly?" Rachel asked. "See if we can have a chat with her?"

Jack shook his head, perhaps a little too quickly. "No, I'll go up on my own. It's going to be full dark by the time we get there and besides," he said with a smile, "you've got work tomorrow."

By the time they reached Rachel's house, the light rain had become a downpour. This, combined with the last of the daylight being lost behind the cloud cover, had turned the evening into night faster than normal.

"Are you sure you want to go up to the Pool tonight?" Rachel asked. She still sat in the car, trying to convince herself that it was only a quick dash across the road and up her path to the front door. "I know I suggested it, but in this weather?"

"The funeral's tomorrow. I'd like to get as much done before then. I don't know why, it just feels important."

"Okay. Wait here a minute." She quickly opened the door and ran out, slamming it behind her as she sprinted across the road . At the door she fumbed with the lock for a second before disappearing inside. Jack watched as lights were switched on in various rooms upstairs, then sat back and waited for Rachel to reappear. When she did, she held an umbrella over her head and a carrier bag in her hand. She opened the door and dropped the bag on the seat, then leaned inside, the umbrella snagging on the door frame, and kissed him.

"There's no rush in getting them back," she said.

"I'll see you tomorrow at the funeral." She kissed him again, then ran back across the road and into her house. When the door was closed, Jack looked into the bag; a torch and a heavy, waxed coat had been hurriedly stuffed inside.

Later, stumbling across the field that connected the woods to the lane, Jack was grateful for the wax coat, which he had pulled on over his own denim jacket. With the last of the grimy daylight hidden behind the cloud cover, it seemed that night had decided to pay an early visit to the hillside above Caerphilly. He trudged on through the mud that had already seeped inside his Doctor Martens somehow, lighting his way with the torch's strong beam until he came to the edge of the woods. Frantically waving the light around, Jack was convinced someone had stolen the head of the path to the Pool until he saw it a few feet off to his left. Cursing the weather and Rachel's idea of coming up here, he stomped over and entered the trees, grumbling at the lack of cover their thin branches afforded him.

Ten minutes later, his legs sore from brambles and thorns, he came out into the clearing and stood on one of the slabs that surrounded it. He knelt briefly, playing the light over the stone and trying to make out any designs cut into it, but if there had been decorations they had long ago been worn away by the weather.

"*Hello, Jack,*" Jo said beside him, making him jump. She stood, wearing the exact same clothes she had worn every time he had seen her, and he was only a little surprised to see the rain falling through her, leaving her as dry and smooth as he remembered from the night before.

"Jo. How you doing?" They stood, awkward and embarrassed. Jack reached for a cigarette before remembering he'd left them at home so as not to bother Rachel. He patted his pockets for a moment, then looked over at the young girl. "I need your help."

"*With what?*" She stepped over to a large log on the edge of the woods and sat down, patting the space next to her. Jack walked across and, in a gesture that reminded him of his brother, tucked the hem of his coat underneath him to prevent his jeans getting wet.

"I need to know more about the Pool. About the Chapel, what they plan to do and how I can stop it."

Jo nodded without looking at him. She waved her hand in front of them and Jack gasped.

As in a movie in which one scene changes into another, the rain soaked woods and Pool disappeared and another version of them took their place; the image was superimposed on the original but the volume was turned off. Jack watched as children splashed and played in the Pool and around it, clearly laughing and shouting and enjoying the hot summer's day that Jo was showing him, but he couldn't hear a thing. The sun streamed through the leaves of the surrounding trees, sparkling with an intensity almost too bright on the surface of the water now filled the Pool-- the water that seemed filled with tiny particles of crystal, too small to touch or hold, yet large enough to glitter and shine, reflecting the sunlight.

Jo nudged him, pointing over to a small girl, perhaps seven or eight, who sat on the edge of the Pool, kicking her feet in the water, giggling as she did so, laughing as the water sparkled around her toes like tiny flies made of diamonds.

"*Look familiar?*" she asked. "*That's me, aged about seven. I used to come up here all the time, every chance I got. I loved it. Swimming and fooling around with my friends. Some of the best times of my life.*" She pointed again, this time to the corner opposite where they sat. As she did so, a huge hulk of a man came out of the woods, wearing only a pair of shorts and a shirt with the sleeves rolled up.

"*That's the Lifeguard. Jennifer Evans had gotten lost in the woods so hewent to find her.*" Jack saw the man was leading a small girl, only about four or five, dressed in a pink swimming costume; one of the girls rubbed at the tears that trickled down her face. The Lifeguard beckoned one of the other, older girls over and gave the smaller child to her, speaking silently all the while.

"That's Jenny's sister, Liz. She was supposed to be watching her but she was having too much of a good time. The Lifeguard gave her a telling off, but not like any adult I'd ever heard before. He didn't shout at her, just told her what she had done wrong and how to change it. Far as I know, Jenny never went missing again when she was with Liz."

"Who was the Lifeguard, Jo?"

She didn't answer him, merely passed her hand in front of them again. The scene shifted once more, but only slightly. It was still a summer's day, the Pool was still full of sparkling water and laughing children, but there were subtle differences. Jack noticed that none of the kids actually had swimming costumes; rather they were wearing either vests and shorts or, in several cases, just their underwear. In some strange way their hairstyles looked different, too, as if they had all been cut using the same scissors and the same bowl.

Standing in the corner, wearing a pair of trousers rolled up to the knees and a white vest, stood the huge Lifeguard, smiling as the kids played.

"*This is in the '40s sometime. Spot the differences?*"

Jack shrugged. "Sure, with the clothes and everything, but -- "

"*But the Lifeguard looks the same. Watch.*"

Again, Jo waved her hand in front of them and again the picture before them shifted. The children and the Pool were still there, but the kids looked dirtier somehow, more unkempt. Many of them had shorts on held up with string, and not a few of them were swimming or standing naked, including some of the older ones.

Standing over them all, like a great sentinel was the Lifeguard. With a string vest over his huge barrel chest, trousers around his legs and a flat hat on his head, he looked exactly the same as he had in the first image Jo had shown him.

"*The 1920s,*" she said.

"Who is he?"

"*I think he may well be your salvation.*" Jack turned to look at her, a question on his lips which died as he saw her eyes, which brimmed with tears that but refused to fall. *"I'm sorry about last night, Jack. I've just been so lonely, I . . . Anyway, make sure you treat Rachel right, Jack. She seems like a really nice girl."*

"Jo?" Jack said, reaching out to touch her. In an eye blink the images of the Pool, the children and Jo herself were gone, leaving him alone in the cold and rainy night. "Jo?" he called into the sky, but was answered only by the wind sliding through the bare branches of the trees.

He drove back to Newport slowly, partly because of the rain, partly to give himself time to think. Smoking one of the cigarettes he'd bought at an all-night garage, Jack sat in his car outside his house, looking at the living room window where a light burned once again. In the last few days his life had turned upside down to such an extent that it would not surprise him if he woke in a lunatic asylum one morning, realising the whole thing had been some form of fevered hallucination.

"It was all a dream," he said to himself, stepping out of the car and heading for his house. He slammed the front door behind him, threw his car keys on the hall table and strode into the living room through the ruined remains of the door, cigarette smoke floating after him like the trail
of a steam train.

"Okay, show yourself," he said to the empty room. "I've got no time for your stupid theatrics tonight. If you're going to haunt me tonight, then do it now." Jack stood in the centre of the room, turning slowly, watching carefully.

With a sound like gas escaping from a burst pipe, a stream of darkness filtered into the room from one of the plug sockets. Slowly it took shape and filled out in the approximate form of a man, yet one without definition, being only a solid, flat mass of darkness. Jack took a step back as it walked over to the sofa which stood between them like a barrier and put its hand on the back of it, leaning forward.

"**Hello, Jack,**" it said, a grin of pure white teeth springing into view in its facial area, shining out at him from the void. "**I was hoping we could talk tonight.**"

Jack stood his ground and stared back at the apparition. "Why?"

"**Tonight will be our last visit, Jack. Tomorrow you will burn your father and his soul will be freed. I shall return to . . . to wait until your brother calls the Body.**"

His hand shaking, Jack quickly stubbed out his cigarette in an ashtray beside one of the chairs, then instantly lit up another from his packet.

"Call the body? What are you talking about?"

"**Your father was offered in sacrifice to the larger Self, to the Body. I am but one part of the Spirit of the Pool. There are others like me, who manipulate the paltry souls of your kind for our own needs.**" Its grin was fixed as it talked.

"But why speak with me? Shouldn't you be haunting Matt?"

"**I have spoken all I wish to Matthew. He be lieves I will claim the Body of the Spirit and use its strength at his bidding.**" The thing chuckled slightly, its head shaking back and forth. "**Yet he will have no claim on my loyalty as he is not the Son of the Sacrifice.**" It leaned closer, the bright grin widening. "**Matthew was born of your mother, but he is not your father's son**."

Jack sat down in the chair, tired beyond belief by everything that he had heard and seen over the last few days; now some sort of demon was telling him that his brother was actually his half-brother. He glanced up at the print above the fireplace, the picture of Don Quixote and Sancho Panza, and felt a rush of empathy with the poor knight. Here he sat in his living room with his very own windmill... and in a few days, he was expected to charge at even more.

"Who are you, anyway?" Jack asked in a tired voice as he turned back to the grinning void.

"I am the Voice of the Body, Jack, the Voice of God. I am a part of the Spirit of the Pool that yearns to be freed from both the Pool and the larger Self."

"And that's what the Chapel of the Locus are going to do on Friday, right? Free you from the Pool?"

The shape stood up as if surprised.

"**You should have contented yourself with the knowledge that the Chapel murdered your father. I merely sought confirmation of that when I . . . visited you last night. Its plans should not concern you**."

Jack blew smoke out.

"Too late," he said. "We know all about you and the Chapel. About the Dreaming Pool and the Life-guard."

"**The Lifeguard is dead!**" the Voice shouted suddenly, its grin changing into a grimace, the white teeth staining blood red. Jack pushed himself back into the chair as far as he could go, his eyes wide, the hair at the nape of his neck standing up on end. The thing stepped around the sofa and walked into the middle of the room, its mass swelling as it loomed over him, towering above him, the grimace now surmounted by a pair of crimson eyes that glowed and flickered as if alive with flame. "**The Lifeguard is no more! His body was left to rot amongst the trees!**" the Voice roared, its hand reaching down and plucking Jack from his seat, pulling him up level with its shining teeth. "**What do you know of the Lifeguard?**" it asked slowly, its speech choked with menace.

Jack gripped the arm that held him, trying to gain purchase, but the skin was smooth, cold and slippery like raw chickenand his fingers constantly slipped. He struck out, punching the Voice in its head, and watched with some glee as the thing rocked back, the eyes closing slightly, before it returned its gaze to him.

"**What do you know of the Lifeguard?**" it asked again.

"Nothing." Jack gasped as the slimy fingers

clamped tighter around his throat. “I know he was killed . . . that’s all.”

The Voice released him, dropping him back into the chair, looking down on him, its mouth reshaping into a grin, the fire in its eyes dying.

“**I will not see you again, Jack,**” it said, stepping around to the doorway it had destroyed the night before. “**You should hope for your sake I will not see you again.**”

As Jack watched, the shape walked out into the hall and was gone.

6: WEDNESDAY

Jack bypassed the visit to his mother's house before the funeral and drove straight to the crematorium where Mr Navarro informed him that he had arrived before everyone else in the "Bradley party". Hanging around outside while someone else's relative was burned to a crisp inside, smoking cigarette after cigarette, Jack couldn't help wondering where Rachel was and whether she was all right.

As he waited in the car park, a collection of cigarette butts gathering on the ground in front of his car, he watched as the family who had been cremating one of their own began to file out: young men with straight backs and slightly bored expressions, complemented by old women whose veils covered their tearful faces, giving them the appearance of Italian widows mourning the loss of another son in some gangland movie. Jack couldn't help but smile at the thought, though his grin died when one of the younger men looked over at him, scowling. He coughed into his hand and turned away, embarrassed, trying to appear nonchalant. When he glanced back, the young man had moved away with his friends or relatives to the second of the two car parks the crematorium boasted.

Rachel pulled up across from him a moment or two later and waved. After locking up her car, she walked over and, looking around quickly, pecked him on the cheek.

"You look good in a suit, Mr Bradley," she said, smiling.

"How you doing?" he asked, holding her hand, staring into her eyes.

"I'm late, I'll tell you that for free. I'll see you inside." She squeezed his hand and turned to leave, then glanced. "For what it's worth, Jack, it's kinda nice to see you without saying you look like shit." She winked at him, then headed inside.

Jack smiled and ditched another cigarette at his feet. As he ground the red embers into the tarmac he considered whether he could quit smoking for Rachel if they became more than friends. He certainly wanted their tentative relationship to grow, to mature into something other than holding hands and sharing occasional kisses, but how serious did he want it to get?

His thoughts were scattered by another car pulling up in the car park. Jack watched as his brother stepped out, long black overcoat blowing in the slight wind, his crew - cut and small round glasses making him look meaner to Jack than he ever had. Matt caught Jack's eye and began to walk over, frowning as Jack pulled another cigarette from his packet and lit up.

"Hello, Jack," he said, holding his hand out. Jack stared at him for a moment, then shook hands. "Apologies for Sunday, I was well out of order." Jack nodded, watching his brother's face for any sign that he knew of Jack's eavesdropping. "The others'll be here soon. I figured you'd come here first, instead of Mum's place." Looking around the place, Matt said "Hard to believe he's gone."

"Yeah," Jack said. He took a deep pull on his cigarette and blew smoke out into the cool air.

"I know, Matt."

His brother looked at him. "Know what?"

For a second Jack thought he was wrong, that every thing he'd learned over the last few days, all the craziness he'd been part of, could all be chalked up to some sort of grief -related stress, that none of it had really happened the way Jack thought and that Matt was in no way involved with a secret society, let alone implicated in his father's death.

Matt smiled slightly, and Jack knew he was right.

"The Chapel, Matt. The detective inspector. Dad's murder. The Dreaming Pool. The . . . thing you're planning to pull out of there on Friday. The Lifeguard. I know it all, Matt."

His brother stared at him from behind his glasses, his eyes squinting just a little as his smile faltered, his lips tightening to become a thin line that could have been drawn on by a pencil. Somehow, perhaps fortified by the previous night's meeting with the Voice, Jack stood his ground, returning Matt's gaze.

"The Lifeguard is dead," Matt said eventually. "And you know fuck all."

Jack shrugged. "I'd like to differ there, if it's all the same to you."

Matt jabbed his thick finger into Jack's chest, leaning forward and staring down at him. He reminded Jack of nothing more than the bullies he had had to deal with in school.

"Listen to me, Jack. You. Know. Fuck. All. You got that? I don't know who you've been talking to over the last couple of days, but I think you'd do well to remember what that guy said in the pub. Remember? He said forget about the Pool. Cremate dad and just get on with your life."

"And I wonder who told him to tell me that, eh?" Jack said, pushing Matt back a step or two and straightening himself up. "Is that why you met him on Sunday? The black guy? You had to pat him on the back for getting his message right. Because it was you who told him to beat me up and deliver the message, wasn't it?"

"Yes," Matt snarled through gritted teeth.

Jack looked at him, all the anger and fight flooding out of him as his brother admitted what he had only just realised. "Why?" he asked lamely.

"These things don't concern you, Jack. Don't get involved."

"Too late for that."

Matt sneered at him and seemed about to answer when another car drove into the car park. A quick glance showed that it held their mother, sister and their two aunts. Matt tugged his tie straight and walked over to help them out of the car, leaving Jack to lean on his own car, smoking his cigarettes.

" . . . and though I never knew Jonathan Bradley, I have talked with his wife Gillian and his children Diane and Matthew, and they have all impressed upon me . . ." Jack half-listened to the vicar droning on about what a good man his father had been. He noticed that his name wasn't included in the list of people with whom the vicar had spoken; he couldn't be certain, but he'd be willing to bet that Diane had deliberately failed to pass on his phone number or address to the man of God. Or maybe the vicar just hadn't had time to meet him Jack thought, realising that his thoughts seemed paranoid.

Glancing around him as surreptitiously as he could, Jack was surprised to recognise several aunts and uncles on his father's side that he hadn't seen for more years than he cared to remember; this was not because of the feud and years of silence that he and his family had gone through, but because most of his father's family lived in or around London, which was hardly just around the corner. Standing as he was in the front pew on the left -hand side, Jack had to restrain himself from smiling and nodding at those relatives who caught his eye; reacquainting yourself with almost forgotten relations during a funeral was perhaps not the best thing to do, he told himself.

" . . . and I'd like to lead you all in the singing..." the vicar was saying. The people around him reached down and picked up their hymn books, some sharing with their neighbours, but Jack merely stood, hands clasped behind his back, staring into space. He did not believe in God, despite, or perhaps because of, what he had seen over the last few days, and he was positive that he was not going to sing praises to something he neither believed in nor liked if it did exist.

From the corner of his eye he saw Diane glare at him, indicating that he should pick up his hymn book. He smiled slightly at her, knowing how it would annoy her, her anger being compounded by her inability to do or say anything to him, and he continued looking out into space as the congregation began to sing. Jack was surprised when he recognised the hymn as "Jerusalem". Although it was only one of many he had been forced into singing in school, it was the only one he remembered, purely because of the line concerning the building of Jerusalem among "dark, Satanic mills". That image had had remained with him for years; without really understanding it he found it strangely sinister during his school days.

Jack wondered whether Father Josef Durer had thought he and his fellows were building Jerusalem when they had constructed Chapel Point near the Dreaming Pool, and if so, what had they considered to be the Satanic mills? If the thing, the shape that had visited Jack the night before had been speaking truthfully and was indeed been the Voice of God, then Jack seriously doubted Jerusalem had been on Durér's mind when he had built the chapel.

The chapel.

Jack's mouth fell open as the thought struck him. He, Camilla and Rachel had tried to find out as much as they could about the organisation known as the Chapel of the Locus, but none of them had bothered to learn about the actual building, the one which had been constructed near the Pool in the late 1830s. He didn't know why it seemed so important, but he knew he had to visit the site, even if the chapel itself no longer existed, and he knew it had to be soon. Friday was the day, or rather, night set for the Chapel to perform their secret rites --whatever they might be-- and still Jack and Rachel had nothing with which to stop them.

Jack spent the rest of the funeral in a state of high anxiety, tapping his foot incessantly, eager to be away and to talk with Rachel. When the coffin containing his father's earthly remains (Jack found himself wondering whether the head had been sewn back on or just placed next to the body to save time and effort) was at last taken through the red curtains by the conveyor belt, Jack embarrassed just about everyone by standing up and hurrying along the aisle to the exit.

He found Rachel standing like an usherette at Death's theatre outside the main chapel. In her sombre dark suit, she stood awaiting the mourners so that she could lead them out to their cars, emptying the place for the next party of grief-stricken family members.

"Jack? What are you doing out here? You should be inside," Rachel whispered.

"The chapel, Rachel. We've got to visit it," he said urgently, looking over his shoulder through the small glass windows set in the doors to the crematorium. His relations were just standing and beginning to file out, most of them offering condolences and words of meaningless encouragement to Jack's mother. "Can we talk? Ten minutes?"

"I can't, I have to help Mr Navarro with -- "

"Is every thing all right here?" Mr Navarro said as he appeared out of his office. "Mr Bradley, may I offer you and your family my sympathies?" he said quietly as he recognised Jack.

"Thanks," Jack said, turning away as if upset. The doors opened and Jack's family began to leak into the hall, many of them still consoling his mother. More than one or two stared at Jack either with curiosity or hostility.

"Mrs Bradley," Mr Navarro said, slipping easily among the mourners to take her arm and leading her expertly away towards the main doors. Instantly Jack turned back to Rachel.

"Can you get tomorrow off?" he whispered frantically. "It's important, Rache."

"I'll see what I can do," she whispered back, moving off into the throng of Jack's family to offer her help support where it was needed. He watched her as she escorted an aunt of his to the waiting world outside where it was raining once again, then reached into his pocket and drew out a cigarette.

"No smoking in here," Matt said, grabbing his elbow and pulling him through the doors. As the rest of his relations went to their cars in preparation for driving back to their mother's house where a small wake had been prepared, Matt hugged his brother tightly, crushing his arms while, wrapping his other arm around his head as if Jack had broken down in tears.

"Now listen to me, little brother," Matt hissed into his ear. "The Chapel and the Pool are none of your fucking business. I tried to get you to leave it alone and maybe I handled that wrong. Fact of it is, I don't give a shit about you or anyone else here. The only reason I'm telling you this is so you don't attempt anything stupid and try to fuck up our plans."

"What --"

"Shut up!" Matt said, squeezing his head tighter. "Do not fuck around with me or mine, Jack. Leave the Chapel and the Pool alone." Without another word, Matt released him and walked slowly over to his car. Jack moaned, rubbing at the side of his head, and staggered over to the wall of the crematorium. As he stood in the drizzle, trying to light his somewhat crumpled cigarette, he saw Diane striding over to him.

"Don' think yew're comin' to the party," she said loudly, making one or two others look over in their direction. "Yew didn' even sing at yewr own dad's funeral." She stood, waiting for some retort, but all Jack could do was blow tired smoke in her face. Diane snorted and walked away, climbing into the lead car. Jack watched as the rest of his relatives drove off, leaving him alone with the building where his father had been burnt.

"I'm glad you don't bother with your family much," Rachel said at his side. "I'm not sure I could get involved with someone with all that baggage."

Jack chuckled, amazed at how just a few words from her could bring him up out of the black mood that had threatened to swallow him.

"Can you get tomorrow off?" he asked her. "I had a thought while I was in there: we know bits and pieces about the organisation called the Chapel of the Locus, right? We know they were given some land and that they built a chapel up by the Pool. We have to try and find that chapel."

"Why?"

Jack stuttered, lost for words. "I'm not sure," he said eventually. "I've just got a feeling that it might be important. Maybe something to do with the Lifeguard?"

"Who?" Rachel asked, glancing at her watch. She only had a few minutes before the relatives of the next client were due to arrive.

"I was haunted or visited by that . . . that thing, whatever it is, last night, and I confronted Matt this morning with stuff about the Chapel. Both times I mentioned the Lifeguard, and both times they went nuts, saying he was dead and that was it."

"Yeah, but who is he?"

Jack took a deep breath. "Last night when I went up to the Pool, I saw Joanne. She showed me . . . scenes of the past."

"Photographs?"

Jack shook his head.

"No, she actually played out scenes of the past as if

she had them on film or something. Anyway, in all of them there was this big bloke who took care of the kids at the Pool and was called the Lifeguard, and in all of these pictures, these clips of the past, the guy looked exactly the same. She showed me stuff from back in the 1920s and this guy looked no different at all."

"And you think he might be up at the chapel?" Rachel said doubtfully.

"I don't know, it's just a hunch. But we have to do something, Rache. This bunch of nutters my brother's in with are planning to raise God-alone-knows-what on Friday night." Jack paused for a moment and stared off into space. "You ever find it weird that we're talking about someone as if she's a mutual friend, yet all the time she's a . . . a ghost?"

Rachel nodded, quiet herself for a while. Then she said, "Listen, I've got to go. Give me a ring tonight and we'll sort tomorrow out, okay? God knows why, but I suppose I'll come with you." She looked around quickly, then kissed him on the mouth. "See you tomorrow," she said and was gone.

"Jack, you're alive! No one's seen you for days; we thought you were dead or something."

"Yeah, well, cremating your father does strange things to you, you know?"

"Oh shit, sorry Jack. I forgot."

Jack laughed down the phone at the sorrow Camilla's voice held, hating himself a little for deliberately causing it.

"That's all right, my dear, no problems. How is everybody?" They chatted about their friends, who had been doing what, with whom and where, Jack catching up on her news without actually telling her much of what had been happening to him.

"So who's the new girl?" Camilla asked, with a smile so big he could hear it in her voice. "Rich saw you and some girl in Scarlett's yesterday looking very intense."

"Just a --"

"Don't you give me that 'just a friend' bullshit, Jack."

Camilla interrupted quickly. "Is she the one from the crematorium that you picked up?"

"How did you know?" Jack asked before the pair of them said "Gareth." Camilla laughed at Jack's exasperation. "Christ, he's got a big mouth.", said Jack

"So is this the one, then? Is Jack I-don't-get-serious Bradley finally going to settle down?"

"Come on, Camilla, give me a break, huh? We're not even really going out with each other yet."

"Yet, eh?" she said, laughing again.

"So has Gareth asked Annie out yet?" Jack asked, quickly changing the subject.

"You know what he's like -- he'll moon around any girl until she shows a bit of interest and then he's off." Jack chuckled in agreement. "So when are we going to meet this mysterious new girl, then?"

"When you get Gareth to ask Annie out for a beer."

"Christ, that means never. Hey, did that info on the Locus Chapel thing do you any good?"

Jack thought for a moment, wondering whether it had or not. "It came in handy," he said eventually. "I'll give you a ring over the next couple of days, okay? Say hi to everyone from me. See you soon." They swapped their goodbyes and hung up, and Jack wandered into his living room. It was strange how the thought of just spending an evening in, watching some banal TV over a couple of cups of tea and a few cigarettes, sounded so appealing to him. In the last week, he reasoned, he had seen and experienced enough weirdness to warrant a night of mediocrity with absolutely nothing to do.

Except phone Rachel, he remembered with a smile.

7: THURSDAY

The phone purred in his hand as Jack clicked open his Zippo and lit another cigarette, the flame shaking nervously. He sat up straight as his mother's phone was picked up, closing his eyes against his sister's harsh, querying "Ello?"

"Diane. It's Jack."

"What the bloody ell do -- "

"Shut up and listen to me," he interrupted. "You don't like me, fine, great, I don't like you either, but I want to talk to Mum for five minutes, all right?" Her angry silence seeped down the phone line and for a moment he thought she was going to hang up. There was a noise in the background, though, another voice.

"Yew don' ave to if yew don' wan'oo," Diane said before Jack heard the handset being snatched from her hand and his mother's quiet voice saying his name.

"Mum," he said lamely, unsure now of what it was he wanted to say. "You okay?" he asked eventually, clutching at conversational straws.

"Not really," she said, sniffing loudly. Jack wondered if she had been crying non-stop for the last week. "What do you want?"

He sighed. "Just to say sorry, Mum. Sorry for all the . . . the hassle I might have caused over the last few years. That's all." With a half-strangled cough, his mother began to cry again. He imagined her in an armchair beside the coal fire, surrounded by her cheap ornaments and tasteless collectibles, and felt tears rise to his own eyes. "Sorry," he mumbled again. In the background, he could hear Diane's voice shouting again, telling his mother to stop talking to him.

"I . . . I have to go, Jack," she said slowly. "Please . . . pop in at some point, eh?"

"I will, Mum. Mum?" For a second he wanted to ask her whether she had ever had an affair, whether Matt was his brother or not, but he couldn't do it. His mother had suffered enough, he reasoned. "I'm sorry," he said again, and hung up.

He looked around at his living room and crushed his

half-smoked cigarette out in one of the ashtrays before rubbing at his eyes, knuckling away the tears that had gathered there.

"What a fucking mess," he said to himself, though he was unsure whether he meant his room or his life.

"So how did you get on?" Rachel asked once they were settled in her living room.

"Well, after I phoned my mother, I spent most of the morning looking through W.H.Smith for an OS map of Caerphilly and the surrounding area, found one, bought it, took it back home and couldn't find a damn thing on it that mentions or even looks like the Pool." Jack sipped at his tea and looked over at Rachel.

"You phoned your mother? How did it go?"

He shrugged. "It was difficult. I didn't know what to say, and she's still choked up over my dad's death." He shook his head. "Weirdest phone call I ever made."

Rachel smiled in sympathy at him then, after a moment's silence, reached for the map which he held out for her. She took it from him, knelt beside the coffee table and opened it up, folding it to the section which showed Caerphilly. Tracing with her finger, she followed the road out of the town centre, up towards Abertridwr, and along the road that connected with the council estate. Going around it, she hit the lane that she and Jack had walked along last Sunday. Cutting over the field next to it, she ran into the woodland area and, as far as she could tell, where the Pool ought to have been marked with some sort of symbol there were only trees.

"You're right, no Pool. And no chapel either. Not even any ruins."

"Hardly surprising." She looked across at him. "According to that book we found in the library, the chapel was made of wood and thatched with straw, remember? Not exactly the best things to leave a permanent mark."

"Even so," she said with a sigh, looking intently at the map as if her gaze could make something appear. She traced the route again but still found nothing. Sitting back in her chair she picked up her own cup of tea.

"There's got to be something up there," she said eventually.

"Only one way to find out," Jack said, hefting the wax jacket Rachel had lent him the other night. She sighed again.

"I'll get my boots."

By the time they had walked along the lane, over the field and through the bramble-choked woods to the edge of the Pool, Jack was breathing hard and calling for a few minute's break. Rachel stared into the bottom of the wide Pool at the nodules and bumps which she could only think of as metallic coral, her nose crinkling in distaste as if she smelt something bad.

"Christ, I've gotta quit doing this," Jack said.

"Smoking?"

"No, breathing." He smiled at her as he straightened up, then took his own look into the empty Pool. "Strange; I only came here once as a kid, but I can't remember the bottom of the Pool looking as bad as it does now. Even with all those bumps and ridges it still looked kind of... beautiful, really."

Rachel looked at him, doubting whether the Pool had ever been anything remotely approaching beautiful. "So, where do we start looking for this ruined chapel, Sherlock?"

Looking around the entire clearing, Jack was confronted with almost the exact same scene on every side: trees and undergrowth choking any other way out of the area except for the small track which had led them here. The only other bit of colour, he was surprised to notice, were the few remaining tatters of blue and yellow plastic which had marked the site of his father's murder. He pointed over to the ragged strips.

"That way I think, Watson." As they walked around the Pool and began to force their way through the foliage that only stubbornly parted for them, Jack asked, "What the hell was Dr Watson's name, anyway?"

"What do you mean?" Rachel paused and fished in her pocket for a hair band, then tied her long hair into a neat ponytail before stuffing it inside the neck of her jacket.

Turning sideways to help ease through the branches, she began pushing against the undergrowth.

"Well, Sherlock Holmes is Sherlock Holmes, right? But Watson is only ever referred to as Watson or Doctor Watson. Didn't he have a first name? Or was he one of those guys whose parents named him oddly and he just grew up to be a doctor? But if that's so, surely he would have been Doctor Doctor Watson."

"Jack?"

"Yeah?"

"Shut up."

Slowly, as if the trees themselves did not want them to enter any further into the hidden area beyond the Pool, the pair managed to fight and claw their way through the unfriendly woods, gaining scratches and cuts across their hands and faces, snagging their jeans on bramble thorns and becoming dirtier with every step from the moss and slime that rubbed off on them. When they broke free of the woods, they stood filthy, gasping and sore on the lip of a small valley.

The ledge they found themselves on extended perhaps ten feet to their left and right, running into yet more trees on the left-hand side and falling away on the right to begin a sloping path that led down the face of the small cliff to the leaf-and-branch strewn floor of the valley some twenty feet below them. As the path petered out, swamped under the countless brown and copper leaves, a small stream flowed out of the left- hand wall, running down the centre of the valley and clearing a natural swath through the autumnal litter. Along the bottom of the valley branches lay half in and half out of the leaves, some rising like the humps of a sea serpent, others bare of bark and pointing up at the sky like the bleached bones of Tolkien's Ents.

"Did you know this was here?"

"Inspired guess," Jack said with a shrug. "Walking in a straight line from the Pool and through my father's murder site. Connecting the points." He turned to Rachel. "Let's go take a look."

Carefully, they walked along the length of the ledge to the point where they could step down on to the sloping, muddy path. Inching their way down, hanging on to the roots that poked through the wall of the small cliff at their side, they finally stood at the bottom, the thick floor of half- rotten leaves and branches stretching before them.

"Great view," Rachel said as she looked around, a frown on her face. "So where do we start?"

"I've no idea." Jack looked at her and smiled. She pointed over to the fast stream that ran off from the end of the path.

"We may as well follow that for a bit. See if we can find anything." She stepped out gingerly on to the leaves, expecting at any moment to plunge through them to her waist as if they were quicksand. Despite her foot sinking up to her ankle, however, the floor beneath her held. She let out a breath she hadn't realised she'd held and began walking beside the stream down the small valley, Jack following slowly behind her.

Walking too close to the stream, Rachel suddenly felt her foot slide out from under her. Though she managed to keep her balance, her boot plunged into the icy water, soaking her foot and ankle before she could stand upright again. She cursed quietly and glared at the stream, and was surprised to find that rolling along the pebbled bed with the leaves and twigs was an almost unending flow of small bones and animal corpses. Usually they were no bigger than a mouse or vole, but the occasional squirrel carcass also drifted by. As she knelt down, a rabbit skull--part of the fur and flesh still clinging to it, one ear twisting in the strong current--rolled up against a large stone and stared at her from empty sockets, its large front teeth and snout poking through the surface of the water, its lower jaw missing. Rachel stood up quickly and walked off.

The stream curved in to the centre of the valley which, some fifteen or twenty feet further on, was closed off by the side walls dropping down quickly. A solid fence of trees and more thorn laden undergrowth formed a neat, natural boundary, with only a small gap for the stream to bubble through.

"Doesn't look like there's much here," Rachel said, stopping and putting her hands in her jacket pockets.

"I think you're right," Jack said, stepping up behind her, surprising her by slipping his arms around her waist and nuzzling the back of her neck. "Shame really," he said, resting his head on her shoulder. "I kinda hoped . . . " He stopped.

"What?"

Jack laughed and let go of her, half-stepping, half-jumping over the stream and running to the left-hand wall, where he pulled aside the branches and roots that either dropped from the trees above or grew through the earth into the air. Behind them, set firmly into the side of the valley, was a large stone square, a heavily rusted ring in the middle. Carved around the ring was a bad representation of a knotted coil of rope.

Rachel hopped over the stream to where Jack stood and brushed aside more of the loose vegetation that covered the stone.

"What do you think it is?" she asked.

"I'll tell you what I hope it is: the Lifeguard."

"How can it be? This thing looks as if it's been here for dozens of years, maybe a hundred or more. Jo said the Lifeguard was alive in her time."

"I know, but . . . " Jack sighed, looking at the stone, toying with the rusted ring that hung from the face of the square as if from a bull's nose. "I reckon we should give this thing a tug anyway, just to find out what's behind it."

"I wouldn't do that if I were you."

They looked behind them quickly, startled by another man's voice. Standing a few feet away, dressed in black jeans and jacket, a smile on his dark face, was the man who had beaten Jack up in the pub almost a week before, the man who had done so on orders from Jack's brother.

"And who the hell are you?" Rachel asked, taking a step closer. The man's smile widened.

"I represent the Chapel of the Locus, Ms Lewis, and I'd advise you not to tamper with that stone."

"Or what?"

The man spread his hands wide, pale palms upwards. "Any manner of things. Probably yourself and Mr Bradley there would go missing for a few days, to be found sometime next week, a long way from here."

Rachel snorted derisively. "You've seen far too many gangster movies, mate."

His smile never straying, the man quickly moved forward over the stream and punched her in the face. Her head rolled backwards and she staggered back a couple of paces, falling on to her backside, clutching her nose.

"Fucking bastard!" she yelled into her hands, tears streaming uncontrollably down her face. Jack stepped in front of her, his hands clenched into fists.

"Come now, Bradley. After the beating I gave you last Friday, do you think you're anywhere near good enough to try me?"

Something beyond the man caught Jack's attention and he stared open-mouthed over his shoulder, his hands relaxing. The black man stood watching Jack's reaction, unsure whether it was genuine or an attempt to divert his attention.

"*LOOK AT ME.*"

Ignoring Jack, the black man slowly turned around to the speaker, his jaw dropping in silent imitation of Jack. Floating in the air, looking down at him, was Jo, her entire body glowing with a pale light, the air around her rippling with heat. Her arms were outstretched as if she were crucified and her face bore a look of fury. "Who are you?" the attacker asked quietly, looking up at her.

As if in answer, Jo's entire body changed. Her thighs swelled enormously before bursting open, muscle, veins and sinew whipping around to flail at him in a shower of blood. Her belly opened to reveal a nest of intestines writhing outward, blood and juices flowing over them as they uncoiled and began their blind search for him. Her T-shirt was torn apart by her ribs as they slid out of her chest, each one growing longer and longer, free of the confines of her body, reaching out toward him like blood-drenched fingers of bone. The muscles and arteries of her arms exploded outward as her thighs had done, wriggling through the air, spraying a dark red rain across the ground. Her head split apart, her mouth widening, the top of her head falling backwards, leaving only a gaping red wound that leaned forward and stared at him.

"God," he whispered, a squirt of urine dribbling down his jeans. His legs crumpled beneath him, dropping him to his knees as he stared up at the abomination that hissed and writhed before him.

"Bastard," Rachel said, swinging the large branch she had picked up from the valley floor and grinning as it connected solidly with the man's head. Without a sound, he fell into the leaves.

When she looked up, Jo had vanished.

The silence was complete: neither Jack nor Rachel spoke, and it seemed that the wildlife itself had fallen silent, waiting as Rachel looked down at the man who lay crumpled in front of her, a thin trail of blood trickling from his ear and over his cheek.

Eventually, Jack stepped over to her and turned her round to face him. He gently wiped away the blood that ran from her bruised nose, using a light touch but still making her wince.

"You okay?" She nodded.

"Is he dead?" she whispered. Jack stared at her for a second, then knelt beside their attacker, taking his wrist and feeling for his pulse. It beat steadily if a little slowly.

"He's alive. He's going to have one fuck of a headache, though." Jack stood and slipped his arm around her shoulders. "Did you see Jo?" She nodded again, but didn't say anything. "Come on, let's go home."

"What about that stone?"

"You look like you could do with sitting down and having a cuppa."

"I'm not getting punched in the face for nothing, Jack. Go and pull on that ring."

Jack smiled and kissed her on the cheek. Going over to the stone, he took hold of the rusted iron ring, braced one foot against the wall of earth beside it and pulled with everything he had.He fell back on his behind as the ring came away in his hand, scattering small bits of stone around him. Rachel laughed at him, then cried out as the effort hurt her nose. Jack looked back at the stone slab in the centre of which was now a small hole, perhaps three inches across.

Jack stood, brushing the dirt and leaves from his jeans, and looked into the hole, wishing he had brought his lighter or a torch with him.

"Give me that branch, Rache." Rache looked at the thick piece of wood she had used as a club and quickly handed it over. She watched as Jack forced one end through the hole, into the cavity beyond. He levered it against the stone, grinning when the front of the slab burst outwards. Moving it around, he repeated the process until most of the stone was covering the leaves at his feet, then stood back and looked inside.

Sitting in the middle of the square chamber, a piece of red ribbon coiled beside it, was a small whistle, grimy and dirty with only patches of its smooth surface showing through. Jack and Rachel glanced at each other before he reached in tentatively, expecting, at any moment, a huge spider to drop from the roof on to his hand and to rush scuttling up his arm. Nothing happened, however, and a second later he held the ribbon up to the light, the whistle dangling at the end of it.

"Should we blow it, do you think?"

"I am not putting that thing in my mouth," Rachel said carefully. Her face throbbed with dull pain, as if every beat of her heart brought another wave of hurt crashing over her head.

Jack took the whistle in one hand and brushed its mouthpiece off, getting rid of as much dirt as possible before he raised it to his lips and blew. His cheeks puffed out as air rushed through the metal to emit a piercing cry that sent a flock of birds up from one of the trees. They screamed indignantly at being disturbed.

Jack and Rachel looked around, half-expecting the hulking form of the Lifeguard to come strolling through the trees, or just to appear in a puff of smoke like a pantomime genie, but only the birds moved. Jack looked across at her, shrugging. "Maybe you have to blow it three times or something?" He took another breath and blew two more sharp notes from the whistle, looking around the small valley as he did so.

Nothing happened.

"What now?" Rachel asked quietly. As if in answer, a groan drifted up from the black man's prone form.

"I think we should leave," Jack said, turning the whistle over in his hands. As he made to walk off, Rachel held his arm, stopping him.

"Jack, I . . . I'm not sure I want to be alone tonight. After all this, you know?" He nodded and held her for a few moments. Then he put his arm around her shoulder and together they followed the stream back up to the path where they would begin to force their way through the woods to the Pool again.

"What are you going to do with that?" Rachel asked as Jack twirled the whistle around his finger on its ribbon. He stopped, letting it swing back and forth like a pendulum from his hand, then handed it to her. She coiled the ribbon around the whistle and slipped it into the back pocket of her jeans. "A memento," she said.

As they left the clearing, Jack paused and turned back. "Thanks, Jo," he whispered to the afternoon sky.

8: FRIDAY

That night at Rachel's request, they had climbed into bed wearing T-shirts and underwear and had simply held each other, Rachel relaxing in his company after the adventures of the afternoon. She had been unaware until that moment of how much the day had taken out of her, despite the strength and courage she had shown in facing their attacker. Eventually Jack had fallen asleep, only to be woken in the early hours of the morning by Rachel kissing him softly, her hand running over his body. He reached for in her in the semi-darkness, and kissed her passionately for a mere second before she drew back with a hiss of pain, clutching her nose. He apologised, drawing her back to him and kissing her neck instead, his lips slowly inching lower as his hands pushed her T-shirt higher.

No words were spoken between them as they each explored the other's body slowly and carefully, taking pleasure in discovering what pleased the other with their lips and tongues and fingers until they had slipped off their remaining clothes. Rachel rolled away from him, on to her stomach, and reached for the bedside table, pulling the drawer out as he stroked her back. They laughed gently together, partly with embarrassment, when he saw she held a condom.

"Okay?" she whispered. Jack nodded. Their lovemaking was slow and soft, Jack moving between her legs for a while as she sighed beneath him, before she stopped him and rolled him over on to his side, sliding herself back against him so that he could enter her from behind, his arms encircling her as she pressed herself to his body.

They dozed when they finished, until Jack woke again. Moving so as not to wake Rachel, he slipped out of her and the bed, and crept to the bathroom. When he returned, Rachel murmured in her sleep and curled up against him. He lay next to her and drifted off to sleep.

In the morning Rachel moved against him, waking up. She smiled at him and kissed his cheek before looking over at the alarm clock. In five minutes it was due to go off, telling her to get up for work, an idea she could not face this morning.

"How you doing?" Jack asked her noticing with a smile tha she held the covers almost up to her neck though her leg was s draped over his.

"Good. You?"

"Very good." They lay on their sides, looking at each other, mentally journeying around this new facet of their relationship, each still unsure of what the other would do. At last the alarm clock rang, forcing Rachel to turn away and switch the thing off before looking back to Jack. "Are you going into work this morning?" he asked.

She reached up and touched her swollen nose. "I don't think so." She laughed. "I can't be much to look at this morning."

"Oh, I don't know." His fingers gently traced the line of her jaw and stroked her neck. "I think you look just fine." She kissed his fingertips, then leaned out of bed, still holding the covers up to her chest, and searched around until she found the T-shirt she had worn at the start of the night. With as much dignity as she could muster, she pulled it over her head with one hand and held on to the sheets with the other. Jack watched with quiet amusement, finding her modesty strange and out of character for someone who was usually so upfront, yet also refreshingly endearing.

When she was covered up, she turned back to him, smiling and blushing slightly as she saw his grin.

"I'm no whiter-than-white virgin, Mr Bradley, which is not to say that I sleep with just anyone, but I do have my modesty nonetheless. Any problems with that?" She poked him in the chest playfully, daring him to answer yes.

"None at all," Jack said truthfully. He watched as she slipped from beneath the quilt, tugging the hem of her already long T-shirt further down her thighs before opening a cupboard and putting on a towelling dressing gown.

"I'm going to have a wash, make us a cup of tea and ›ne in sick for work. If you'd care to join me in the kitchen, ·e's another dressing gown in here." She blew him a kiss, cing as she tapped her own nose with her fingers, then led out towards the bathroom.

'ack lay in bed a moment longer until he heard the click bathroom door lock. Stepping over to the cupboard that l had indicated he stood and stared at the dressing gown ·ing before him. A few minutes later, Jack stood in the kitchen doorway, hands on hips, and a wry smile on his face, waiting for Rachel to turn around from where she was making tea. When she did so, she immediately started laughing at him. He was wearing a pink and pale yellow silken robe that fell to the middle of his thighs; his white and hairy legs stuck out like thick roots beneath it while the top half failed to close across his chest.

"I'm so glad I can make you laugh," Jack said as Rachel began to calm down. "I think it's rather fetching."

Rachel shook her head. "It's not that. It's just that I meant the other dressing gown." Jack looked at her blankly. "There's another one of these in the cupboard," she said, indicating her own towelling robe with a grin.

Jack picked up his cup of tea.

"Well, I like this one." He hung around on the sidelines as Rachel made them both a breakfast of poached eggs on toast, a bowl of cereal and a glass of ice-cold orange juice. Though he felt guilty thinking of it, Jack couldn't help but remember the plate of toast he had made as breakfast for the girl last week, the one he'd met at a party before all this madness had begun and whose name he couldn't for the life of him keep in his head.

They sat at the table together on the same bench, lazily tucking into their food.

"Any hassle off your boss?"

"It's an answering machine this early. I just said I had a big head cold and wouldn't be in over the next couple of days." Jack looked up at her and smiled, quickly returning to his breakfast. "What?" asked Rachel

Smirking, he said, "It's just that, what with your bruised nose and everything, I'm just kinda tempted to have a little revenge and say you look like shit, that's all." He flinched as she slapped the back of his head, making him yell and drop his fork.

"You can do the washing up for that remark."

"Hey, come on, how many times have you said it to me this week?"

"I'm a lady, I can get away with it. You're not, therefore you can't."

"What's that, sexist feminism?"

"Better believe it," Rachel said, handing him her plate onc she'd finished. Grumbling, but still kissing the top of her he as he stood, Jack took the dishes over to the sink and washed them . She watched him for a while, drinking her tea slowly. “What do you think is going to happen tonight?” she finally said.

Drying his hands, Jack sat next to her, straddling the bench so that he could look straight at her.

“I’m not too sure. Hopefully, we’ll be able to stop these guys before they do whatever it is they’re planning.” He sighed. “Sadly, I’m not sure what it is we’ll be able to do to stop them.”

“Why don’t we get someone else involved? The police or someone?”

“If some detective inspector is part of this Chapel group, I wonder how many other coppers are involved? No, if we were going to talk to someone we should have done it before now. *I* should have done it. No one’s going to believe there’s a group of guys about to raise a demon or whatever at some old pool in the woods. Christ, I’m not sure I believe it, even after all the weird shit I’ve seen over the past week.”

“So we just go up there and see if we can stop them?”

Jack stared at her. “Looks like it.”

“We could get killed, you know? They could actually kill us.”

“I know.”

Rachel leaned against him as he put his arms around her and they held each other for a while.

“Hello, Gareth.”

“Jack! Jesus, where’ve you been?”

“Oh, here and there, you know me.” Jack sat in Rachel’s hallway, fully dressed now, her telephone held between his cheek and shoulder, his fingers idly twirling the spiral cord. “How’s things with you?”

“So-so, you know.” There was a pause as Jack fought to of something to say, and then Gareth added, “Jack, it’s nine o’clock in the morning? What the hell are you up at nine, let alone ringing me?”

‘Listen, Gareth . . . this is really odd. I’ve gotta go off o something this evening and I’m not sure when I’ll be

So you want me to look after the house for you?” said. “No problem, you know that.”

"Well, there is that, but . . . I really don't know whether I'll be back at all."

"What do you mean? Are you in some sort of trouble or some thing?"

Jack sighed. "You could say that, mate. Chances are this is me just worrying over nothing, you know?" he said with a false laugh that died in his throat.

"Jack, what's wrong? Can I help at all?"

"No, I'm sorry, mate. All being well, I'll give you a ring to-morrow, okay?"

"And if you don't? What am I supposed to do then?"

"If you don't hear from me by Monday . . . well, just say goodbye to Camilla and Kate and everybody, okay? Christ, that sounds melodramatic, doesn't it?"

"Jack, don't do this to me."

"Hey listen, just one more favour, okay? You know Annie, Camilla's friend who was up the pub last Saturday."

"Yeah?" Gareth asked, thrown off track by the change of sub-ject.

"Even if you don't get a phone call from me tomorrow, just do me one favour: ask her out tonight. Get her number from Camilla, or phone Camilla and make sure she takes Annie with her to the pub tonight and you make sure you ask her out. Take her to TJ's or something, anything. Hell, you can take her back to my place if you like. You've got the spare keys, yeah?"

"Well, yeah, but --"

"No buts, Gar; you ask Annie out. Don't get drunk to do it either. Don't make an arsehole of yourself. Just talk to her, buy her a couple of drinks and ask her out, okay?"

"Jack --"

"Okay?"

"Okay. But you give me a ring tomorrow, right?"

Jack closed his eyes, hating to hear the scared and pleading tone that lay half hidden in his friend's voice. "I'll try my best, mate, that's all I can say. You take care, all right? Say hi to everyone. Cheers, Gareth."

Jack hung up the phone, wondering whether he had just severed the last contact he would ever have with his life at home, wondering whether he was going to survive the coming night and whatever it was dragging with it. He sat in the hall until Rachel came out of her bedroom, a sealed envelope in her hand, the remains of tears in her eyes.

"I couldn't bear ringing my mum," she said, holding up the letter. "If we don't get back, she'll find this in the kitchen." She leaned against the wall, looking down at him. "Makes it seem a lot more real, doesn't it? We can talk about Jo and her being a ghost and secret societies and everything, but writing this . . . writing as if I'd never see her again . . . Christ, that's the scariest thing of all." Rachel sniffed, looked around at nothing, wiped her nose on the sleeve of her gown and hissed at the pain, laughing at Jack's half-smile before she walked slowly to the kitchen, letter in hand.

The day crawled along. The hands of the clock seemed almost unable to haul the weight of the entire day behind them, dragging the minutes as if they were hours. Jack and Rachel spent most of the morning wondering exactly what it was that they were going to do that evening, how they were going to stop the Chapel of the Locus from doing whatever they were planning. Jack had heard Matt say that the ceremony was to be performed at night, perhaps partly to prevent anyone from the estate catching a glimpse of them. Jack and Rachel agreed to go to the Pool at around five o'clock, giving them plenty of time to find a suitable hiding place, somewhere near enough that they could see and hear what was going on at the Pool but obviously well out of sight.

Jack couldn't help wondering if they were doing the right thing. Maybe Rachel was right: maybe it wasn't too late to tell someone else, someone in authority, someone who could take the responsibility away from them. But even as he had the thought, Jack hung his head. There was no one. If Matt and his cronies had the police in their pocket, as it seemed reasonable to think, then there was nobody around who could do anything. He and Rachel had done all they could but they had been forced into this final showdown . They had even followed up Jo's Lifeguard suggestion and nothing had happened, except that Rachel had gotten smacked in the face and their attacker had been knocked unconscious.

Rachel walked into the living room, thrusting the torch into the rucksack that sat on the sofa. "What's up?" she asked Jack, who looked pensive

"How did we get into this, Rache?"

"From what you've said, it seems your brother killed your father which in turn allowed some sort of demon to haunt you." She smiled. "Sounds a bit stupid when you say it out loud, eh?"

"Do you know anyone who could help us?"

She sighed, sitting next to him and staring at the wall, her hand on his thigh. "I think my uncle would have if he was alive. He was always telling me ghost stories and stuff. It wouldn't surprise me if he believed in them himself; my family always said he was a bit of a nutter, a bit unstable. I liked him, though." She smiled over at Jack. "Probably why I'm going out with you."

"So I'm a bit unstable, am I?"

"Well, I've never gotten involved with someone who dropped me into a situation like this before."

"You've got a point."

She stood up, looking at the clock. It was nearly twelve. "Come on, Mr Bradley. We should eat before our great adventure."

Despite his protestations about not being hungry, Jack ate the simple meal that Rachel cooked for them and only grumbled once or twice when she made him wash up again afterwards. They whiled away the afternoon trying to think of anything else they might need for the evening's expedition. At the same time, they swapped stories about childhood and their friends, filling up the time before their departure by subconsciously trying to get to know each other as quickly as they could. The thought that they might not return from the Dreaming Pool, however, always bubbled beneath the surface of their minds, occasionally breaking upwards, a grey thought cutting through their conversation like a shark fin. Suddenly they realised it was half past four. One moment they had been eating their lunch, the next it was time to leave, as if the clock had somehow speeded up when their attention was distracted.

"I suppose we'd better get to it then?" Jack said.

"I suppose so." Rachel stood and double-checked everything they had packed in her rucksack. "If these guys don't turn up until midnight or something, we're going to have a long and probably uncomfortable wait."

"I'd rather spend a few hours lying on branches and thorns with you than turn up just as they're halfway through things and end up as some sort of sacrifice."

"Do you think they'll actually have a sacrifice?" Rachel asked quietly. Jack stopped at the door, running his hand through his hair.

"I don't know," he said after a moment.

They took Rachel's car as a safety precaution, in case Jack's was seen and recognised by Matt. Nothing was said between them during the drive up to the estate. Once on foot - through the lane, across the muddied field and into the woods -- both of them listened for anything that sounded out of the ordinary. With almost every step they looked over their shoulders to see if they were being followed, as they had been the day before, while at the same time trying to look ahead in case anyone was already at the Pool. By the time they reached the stone slabs that formed the Pool's perimeter they felt sure they were the only people around.

"Where are we going to hide?" Rachel asked, looking around at the tangled undergrowth that choked the bases of the trees on every side. She glanced up, wondering for a moment if the branches could support them; one look at the spindly limbs removed that idea.

"I reckon we should push through there," Jack said, pointing off to the trees on one side of the Pool, "and see if we can flatten enough space for the blanket. We should be able to watch what's going on from there."

Rachel followed Jack to the place he had indicated midway along the right-hand side of the Pool, and watched as he began to trample and crush the undergrowth beneath him, forming a rudimentary path into the trees. "Aren't they going to see this?" she asked.

"If it's dark enough by the time they get here, hopefully they won't be able to. Plus they're probably going to be concentrating on their nice little ceremony."

Jack chose an area behind two trees that stood close to each other, giving them a view of the Pool through the space between the trunks while at the same time offering cover. The pair of them wandered around, crushing and flattening the weeds and brambles beneath their feet before they spread first one and then a second blanket on top of them, the first not being thick enough to prevent the spikes and splinters from poking through. Sat with their backs to the trees behind which they were hiding, the third blanket spread over their legs, Jack and Rachel settled down to wait.

If it were possible, the evening seemed to wander past at an even slower rate than the morning had. Jack and Rachel talked for a while, more to pass the time than for any other reason, swapping opinions of books and films they'd enjoyed, TV shows they'd watched and bands they had seen. After a while they merely sat, and thought, looking out into the woods, until first Rachel and then Jack drifted off in an uneasy sleep.

They woke some time later, not to the sound of people arriving but to the heavy pat-pat-pat of raindrops falling through the branches above them. The large drops quickly became a down pour that soaked through their blankets and clothes in no time at all.

"Fucking typical," Jack muttered as he and Rachel pulled the top blanket up over their heads, trying to form a roof to keep the worst off them; unfortunately the heavy wool merely soaked up the rain and let it slip through its fibres, creating a mini waterfall between them.

"This is not an ideal date, Jack."

"Tell me about it." The woods were dark now; a look at her watch showed Rachel it was almost ten o'clock . Aside from the trees and bushes immediately surrounding them, Jack and Racel could see nothing at all, not even the Pool or its clearing. When something moved through the undergrowth off to their right, they both jumped; the thing, whatever it was, ran through their makeshift camping area, uttering a short bark into the night.

"What the fuck was that?" Jack asked, looking around madly.

"Probably a badger or a fox," Rachel whispered, pulling the blanket back above them although it did no good. The down-pour continued and it wasn't long before their legs were soaked through from above and below, the rain collecting in a puddle beneath them. They squatted on their heels for as long as they could before their muscles started to complain. No sooner had Jack stood up to stretch his legs, however, than Rachel pulled him back down.

"Thought I heard something," she hissed. The pair stared through the space between the two trees, straining to see or hear anything from the direction of the Pool. Time stretched out again, the beat of the rain on their heads and backs seeming to repeat endlessly as if the two of them were frozen in the same split second.

"Through here," called a voice from the path. Instinctively Jack and Rachel ducked down, while continuing to peer through the darkness. Suddenly a light became visible, a torch being carried along the path. More lights joined it until a procession of lights was making its way to the Pool; their beams showed figures in heavy coats trampling over the roots and foliage on the ground.

Perhaps a dozen people crowded into the clearing, their boots splashing through the small puddles that had collected on the stones around the Pool. They split up into groups and postioned themselves at the sides of the pool and each corner, then took rucksacks off their backs and knocked eight wooden stakes into the earth. Halogen lamps were lit, turning the entire Pool area into daylight: the lamps were placed on top of metal rods which in turn were placed on to the wooden stakes, metal cages at the bases of the rods holding them in place. Jack stared at the members of the Chapel and thought of the picture in his living room, of Don Quixote charging at the windmills he was convinced were giants. He doubted whether these giants would prove to be as harmless as the poor knight's delusions.

"Well done, ladies and gents." one of the men said, pushing back his hood and closing his eyes as the rain cascaded over his face. Jack cursed quietly as he recognised his brother. Matt opened his mouth wide and flung his arms out, gargling with the rainwater before spitting it out into the Pool with a laugh. "Peter, Tim, if you'd be so kind..." he said to two of the men. They took up their torches and walked around the Pool slowly before crashing through the bushes directly in front of Jack and Rachel.

"Shit!" Jack said. He turned to run but his cramped legs spilled him on to the soaking blankets. Rachel hauled him up and tried to pull him into the woods before one of the men grabbed a handful of her hair, yanking her backwards and pulling her to the ground. The other kicked Jack in the back, sending him sprawling into a bramble bush. It was only a matter of moments before they were dragged out into the clearing around the Pool.

"Hello again," the black man said to Rachel as he pushed back his hood, a bandage, brilliant white against his dark skin, wrapped around his head.

"So good of you to join us, little brother," Matt said with a smile as Jack and Rachel were forced to kneel at the Pool's side. "Poor old Tim's been watching you for hours, you know. He's as wet as you are." He looked over his shoulder at one of the other men. "Detective Inspector, meet my brother Jack." The policeman grinned and waved .

"What are you going to do with us?" Rachel asked.

"Ah, the eternal question of the hostage." Matt paused, looking at her. "You were at my father's funeral, weren't you? Do you work for the crematorium?" Rachel nodded. "Then you should be no stranger to death, my dear, which is just as well because that is what's going to happen to you." He spread his arms as if in apology. "Can't raise a demon without a sacrifice now, can, we?" Matt turned back to Jack. "I believe you know another of our merry little band?" He nodded his head toward two of the others standing at the head of the Pool who had revealed themselves to be women by pulling their hoods back. Jack groaned as he recognised one of them.

"Small world, eh Jack?" Eve said, her lips a tight thin line.

Matt smiled at his brother. "Trust me, Jack; it was no coincidence Eve was at that party a week ago. She's been keeping an eye on you all week." He sighed and brushed some of the rain off his face. "'Course, she's not the brightest of girls, but. . ." He shrugged.

"Just how clichéd can you be, Matt?" Jack asked. His brother knelt down beside him and patted his cheek in a companionable manner.

"Just how fucked can you be, Jack?" He stood and clapped his hands a couple of times. "Okay people, let's get ready."

As the other members of the Chapel busied themselves around the Pool, Jack and Rachel's hands were tied up with what felt like a plastic line, Jack's hands tied to Rachel's feet and vice versa. They were left kneeling back to back beside the Pool in the pouring rain, shivering with cold and dread.

Jack watched as Matt, Eve and the other woman put together a sort of DIY lectern, slotting pieces of wood together and covering the top with a curved plastic shield. From within his coat, Matt produced a slim book and quickly placed it on the lectern so that it wouldn't get wet. He flicked through it until he found the right page.

"Where's your robes and incense, Matt?" Jack called. "Surely you need an altar with pentagrams and candles and a couple of virgins?"

His brother smiled but didn't look at him. "This is the twentieth century, Jack. The Chapel of the Locus has survived by adaptation. Despite your claims of clichés, we have progressed."

"You call killing your own father progress?"

"His death was necessary for the ceremony." He looked up at the sky and quoted, "Take your father, your only father, whom you love, and offer him as a sacrifice at the place that I shall show you." Matt smiled at Jack. "The Gospel according to Josef Durer. Dad's death opened the pathway to the Pool and what lies beneath it. What we shall very soon raise from it."

"Why are you doing this?" Rachel called over her shoulder, her back to Matt and the lectern.

"Why else? Power."

"What if you weren't Dad's son?" Jack asked.

"Excuse me?"

"What if you were illegitimate? What if mum had an affair and you were the result? You ever wonder why your Pool demon haunted me and not you? You're not the Son of the Sacrifice, Matt."

Matt glanced over at Tim. "Shut him up, would you?" With a malicious grin, Tim walked over and kicked Jack hard in the back again, sending pain rolling through his kidneys, leaving him groaning and gasping for breath, his tears mingling with the rain that continued to fall. "Now, if we're all ready?"

With the other Chapel members arranged in groups at each corner of the Pool, Matt began reading from the book.
He coughed up harsh, guttural words from his chest that

seemed to contain too few vowels, like a strange mixture of German, Welsh and Latin; they mixed with the rain and fell heavily on the stones around him. The sounds seemed to stain the slabs with their ugliness before oozing into the Pool itself.

The Pool moved, the surface rippling slightly as something stirred beneath it. Rachel nudged Jack, forcing him to look up from the foetal position he had curled into. Before them the floor of the Pool churned, the coral rocking back and forth, sliding over itself and grinding together, cracking away from the sides. Tendrils of darkness poured out through the gaps, stretching out to touch the night air as the centre of the Pool raised itself up. A gigantic tearing sound was wrenched from the earth as the thing turned this way and that, breaking free of the last of its bonds until it stood, the coral of the Pool forming a hard shell that rode upon the back of its dark mass. It wavered uncertainly in the light of the lamps, light that revealed nothing of its shape or form except its vastness; the huge, rolling thing seemed to stretch and move as if tensing muscles the size of trees. It had no face, no features, only the rippling coral that covered one side of it giving it a front and back. As it stood in the rain and the wind, it roared, the sound of a escapee reaching freedom, the cry of a new born.

"Oh fuck," Jack whispered.

The mass shifted, its bulk turning slightly, twisting to one side, and as Jack felt its attention bear down on him as if it had a physical weight, an eye opened in the darkness, huge and lidless, the white circle stark against the blackness in which it swam, the pupil fluctuating as it focused, staring down at him.

"**We know you. Our Voice has spoken with you,**" it thundered, the words falling upon him harder than the rain that still emptied on to the whole scene. The thing reached out with a portion of its mass, the darkness funnelling into the shape of an arm, three huge fingers sprouting at the end, gripping Jack as he leaned away from its grasp and lifting him into the air. Rachel screamed in shock and pain as the plastic cord tightened around her wrists and ankles, Jack echoing her cry as he took her weight; Rachel spun and dangled beneath him as he stared into the single eye that swivelled and moved as it glared at him. "**You are the Son of the Sacrifice. Our Voice remembers you.**"

"They are food for your sustenance!" Matt shouted up at it, a self-satisfied smile on his face. "We have brought them for you." The eye in the darkness swung around to stare down at him, the pupil shrinking almost to nothingness, then widening to almost entirely fill the white. Jack and Rachel were flung from the hand that held them, the arm disappearing back into the body of the mass as they dropped into the bushes and branches that littered the edge of the clearing. With a sharp crack Jack's arm broke, and he screamed once before falling silent.

"**We do not know you.**" the shape said to Matt; several smaller eyes sprang to the thing's surface, each one white and shining, the full force of its gaze brought to bear upon him.

"I am the Bishop of the Chapel of the Locus and I speak only to the Voice of the Spirit," Matt shouted out to it, spreading his arms wide as if to balance himself against the awful presence that stared down at him. "I am the Son of the Sacrifice. It is my calling that you now answer. It is my boon that you will grant."

The massive body paused for a moment, the largest eye retreating into the dark mass to be replaced by two crimson orbs that glowed with the fires of damnation. One by one, the smaller eyes blinked and turned red as the Voice that had tormented Jack filled the entire Body.

"**Hello, Matthew. You should have listened to your half-brother. You are not the Son of the Sacrifice. We know this.**" Matt stared, his smile faltering. Around him, the other members of the Chapel looked at each other. "Something's wrong," Rachel heard Peter say. "Oh Christ," another person muttered.

Beneath the eyes that spun and moved to look at every member of the Chapel a huge grin spread displaying row upon row of triangular teeth, each one reflecting the white light from its serrated edges. With the sound of cracking whips, tendrils snapped forth from the darkness around the mouth that had opened and wrapped themselves around Matt's body, tossing aside the lectern and the book, lifting him upwards. He screamed only once, a plaintive cry of denial, as he was pulled into the waiting maw. The teeth sliced down on his wriggling form, biting him in two, and his legs and midriff were casually dropped by the side of the Pool where the remains of his guts spilled out on to the stones, blood and viscera cascading down into the darkness that now filled the bottom of the Pool.

Rachel heard the other members of the Chapel scream. They bolted for the path as black tendrils exploded from the creature's body and wrapped themselves around legs and arms, drawing them inexorably towards the thing that waited in the Pool. Its eyes scanned everything as more mouths opened in its mass, teeth shining in the light of the lamps as they ground against each other, millstones waiting for the grist. One of the women, her arms held by the thing, slipped out of her coat and ran into the woods, crashing through the trees and undergrowth, into the darkness. The black man, Peter, uttered a sharp squawk as a glistening, shoelace-thin tentacle whipped around his neck, barely giving him time to struggle before he was pulled into the waiting tooth-filled darkness. The detective inspector was the only Chapel member who fought against the creature, drawing a pistol from inside his coat and firing shots at the thing before he too was dragged screaming into one of the hungry mouths, the teeth slicing him in two as they had all the others, his legs and abdomen discarded to bleed into the woods or on to the stones.

One by one the eyes in the body of the creature winked out, like stars being covered by clouds, until only the flickering red eyes remained: they looked about until they fixed on Jack and Rachel, huddled at the edge of the trees.

"You should not have come here, Jack. I told you we should not meet again."

Rachel nudged Jack, who moaned and looked around, his eyes glazed and unfocused. She cursed, her hands pulling at the cord that connected them, rubbing against a small, hard bulge in her jeans. The Voice stared down at them patiently, the scaly covering that had been the floor of the Pool twitching occasionally as if the creature were uncomfortable with it.
As Jack's head rolled uncontrollably, blood from a head wound running down the side of his face, Rachel scrabbled in her back pocket as best she could, snagging the piece of ribbon she found there. She nudged him again, feeling panic as the eyes turned to her, the grin beneath them spreading. Finally she pulled the whistle from her pocket, wondering how she was going to blow

it.

"If only he was aware of his powers and privileges as the Son of the Sacrifice. In this state, he is merely meat. As are you."

Rachel flicked her wrist, sending the whistle on to the rain -soaked slabs. Glancing quickly at the eyes, she braced herself and pulled Jack to the side, the pair of them landing on their arms. She winced as Jack's head smacked on to the stone.

"You are struggling. Good."

Rachel arched her neck, coughing out the rain she swal lowed as she tried to snatch the ribbon between her teeth, the thin red material seeming to almost deliberately elude her. The Voice watched for a moment, its head cocked to one side like a dog's. Rachel grunted as she pushed herself closer to the ribbon, biting down on it and pulling the whistle to her.

"No more struggles. Those times are over now, child." Rachel spat the ribbon out as soon as the whistle was in reach, grasped the silver metal between her lips and blew as hard as she could, the clear sound searing the night sky. The Voice reached out its huge, three-fingered hand again, but halted as a single light shone from the head of the Pool, brighter than the halogen lamps, illuminating the trees, pushing back the night. The dark bulk turned to the glow and watched a figure step lightly through the woods, unhindered by the plant life, until she stood where the lectern lay in ruins.

"Who are you?"

"You know who I am."

The whistle fell from Rachel's mouth. "Jo?" she whispered. Jo turned to face her, a smile on her shining face. It was Jo's voice, Jo's smile, but her body had changed beneath her cropped T-shirt and denim cut-offs, becoming filled out, lean yet muscular as if untold strength lay beneath her skin. She looked back at the hulking shape in the Pool still smiling.

"I am the Lifeguard. Relinquish your claim to the Body and return to your true position." She held out her hand and, as Rachel watched, a strand of light with as little substance as a moonlit spider's thread slipped from her fingers and touched the darkness before her. The Voice roared only once--a cry of pain and frustration--the red eyes and tooth filled mouths quickly vanished into the Body, replaced with the single eye that had

originally surfaced. *"Do you know what is to happen?"* Jo asked the creature.

"**We are to become unformed. You will be Our Guardian**." Jo nodded. "**Our Voice wishes to remain in this world. The Chapel of the Locus has spoken with it. It . . . wishes to be apart from Us. It has changed. Yet it cannot exist without Us.**"

"The Chapel offered your Voice freedom from you if it would tell them how you could be raised and controlled. In malice, the Voice used the spirit of Jonathan Bradley to terrorise his son. Knowing the Bishop, Matthew, was not the Son of the Sacrifice, it told him how to raise your form from the Pool, hoping to control you long enough to destroy them."

"**We do not understand.**"

Jo smiled kindly. "*I know. I will stop others waking you. I should have prevented this. I shall do better.*"

The thing shifted again, its eye looking around at everything one last time as if trying to remember as much as it could, and then the darkness of its body flowed around it, taking it back into itself. Slowly, with Jo and Rachel watching in silence, the Spirit's Body folded in on itself, collapsing into a smaller form, shrinking down, the shell on its back turning and twisting into new shapes as it became level once more with the floor of the Pool, the coral melting, running into the cracks that were left, sealing them up until everything lay as it had at the beginning of the evening.

Jo stepped over to where Rachel and Jack lay, and knelt beside them to untie their bonds.

"Jo, what the hell happened? Why didn't you kill that thing?"

She picked up the whistle and slipped the ribbon over her head, the whistle resting just above her breasts. "*Not everything must end in violence, Rachel. The Pool Spirit is like a child. It does not understand a great many things. As for Jo,*" she said with a smile, "*I am more than Joanne Daniels. I retain aspects of Jo, but I am the Lifeguard. As the Lifeguard, I am not here to keep the Spirit from escaping. I am here to prevent people trying to release it. I have returned the Dreaming Pool to its original state and shall not allow this to happen again.*" She took hold of Jack's head gently, turning it to the light. "*He is hurt. You should take him to a place where he may be cared for.*"

"What about you?" Rachel said, rubbing at her aching wrists and ankles, where bruises had already blossomed. Jo indicated the clearing and the woods that surrounded it, frowning at the number of ravaged bodies that littered the area.

"*This is my home. I have much to do.*" She helped Rachel stand, then lifted Jack so that he could lean on Rachel for support. "*You should go.*"

Stumbling with the weight of him, Rachel guided Jack along the stone slabs and towards the path. She paused at the entrance to the woods, the rain still falling on everything, and looked back. The Lifeguard stood watching her. With a nod, Rachel turned and led Jack out of the trees.

9: SATURDAY

"So it's over?"

"Seems that way." Rachel sat on the edge of Jack's hospital bed, looking down at him. She smiled faintly at his head swathed in bandages and wondered if he knew about the bald patch the nurses had had to shave to get at the gash in his scalp. His left arm lay in plaster, suspended by wires and pulleys, his bruised fingers poking out at the end. Her own wrists and ankles were bandaged, and one of the nurses had told her that her back looked like a painting by Francis Bacon. Jack listened in silence as Rachel described the deaths of the Chapel members, and told him about Jo and her transformation.

"I know it's corny to say this, but everything happened so fast. One minute we're surrounded by nutters, the next . . . Jesus, Jack, you ought to be glad you missed it all."

"I'm sorry you had to go through it on your own." They looked at each other, unsure of what to say next.

"Oh, but she didn't." The cold blade of a scalpel pressed against Jack's neck, rasping along his stubble. Rachel leapt up and looked at the woman who had sneaked up on them. Her jeans and jumper were filthy and appeared to be damp; her face was bruised and scratched and twigs stuck up from her hair; and the hand that held the scalpel was covered in dirt and dried blood.

"I was there as well."

"Eve?" Jack whispered, hardly daring to move. She looked down at him and slipped the blade along his skin, shaving off a few hairs.

"You remember my name when I pull a fucking knife on you, don't you?" she hissed. She looked across at Rachel. "Sit down." Her hands clenched into fists, Rachel sat on the hard plastic chair and glanced quickly around the room. No one else seemed to be paying them any attention, not even the couple visiting the guy in the next bed.

Eve leaned over Jack and a small brown leaf fell on to his chest from her hair. "I spent the night in that fucking forest, Jack," she whispered. "I tried and tried to get out, but that bitch of a Lifeguard wouldn't let me leave. She kept me going round and round and round . . . I wanted to lay down and die, but she wouldn't even let me do that." Eve quickly switched the scalpel to her other hand, and held it tightly against Jack's cheek, the tip of the blade millimetres from his eye.

"Eve?" he said quietly.

"Shut up! I could have been somebody special. I could have been ruling most of fucking Europe by this morning if it hadn't been for you, and now look at me!" She stood up, her arms spread wide. "I look like a fucking scarecrow!" she shouted. Almost instantly, a nurse stepped over to her.

"Keep the noise down --"

Eve slashed out with the scalpel, the metal slicing into the nurse's uniform, gashing her arm.The nurse shrieked and took a step back, before collapsing as Eve grabbed a water jug and smashed it into her face, water erupting everywhere. Eve grabbed Jack by the bandages on his head, put the blade once again to his throat, and looked around wildly.

"I was going to be someone special!" she cried. "Now look at me!" Her bottom lip trembled and she sniffed, fighting back her tears.

"Eve," Rachel said quietly. The other visitors had moved away from the patients' beds and she could dimly hear an alarm ringing. Someone carefully picked up the stunned nurse and pulled her away from the bed. Jack lay very, very still.

"Eve," she repeated. "Did you see what happened last night? After the Voice took everyone?"

"I saw that bitch the Lifeguard. She ruined everything same as you two."

"Did you hear what she said to me?" Rachel reached out very slowly and held Jack's hand. He gripped it tightly. Around them, everything was quiet. Rachel was aware of two nurses standing with the patients and their visitors, hovering uncertainly. Eve nodded.

"Not everything has to end in violence, Eve. Things wouldn't have worked out anyway, even without us and the Lifeguard. Matt was wrong. He couldn't control that thing. He never could. There was nothing you could have done. It wasn't your fault, or ours." Eve blinked, tears running through the grime on her face. Rachel smiled gently at her and took her hand, lifting the knife away from Jack's throat.

"It doesn't have to end in violence, Eve." As Rachel took the scalpel from Eve's fingers, the two nurses stepped forward. Eve began to sob and weep hysterically, collapsing in on herself, trying to fold up into the foetal position. "Come on, love," one of the nurses said not unkindly, and lead her away.

"You all right?" the other nurse asked both Jack and Rachel. They nodded. "I'll be back in a moment," she said, and followed her colleague.

"Fuck," whispered Jack, then looked up at Rachel.
"Thanks," he managed. Rachel smiled.

"You look like shit." Jack said nothing, but reached out and pulled her close. Heedless of the stares of the other people, Rachel bent forward and kissed him gently on the lips.

At the top of a hill, above the Dreaming Pool and sheltered within the trees gathered around it, lay a small open space, only a foot wide. In the centre of this space surrounded by five small stones that poked up from the ground like the fingers of some buried troll, was a small hole that burrowed deep into the hill. As the day drew to a close, the grass overlapping the hole's entrance blew upward as some silent and invisible wind wormed its way to the surface. Dimly, the sound of bubbling water could be heard.

The grass around the hole fluttered for a minute or two until a mixture of mud, leaves and water came to the top, carrying with it the small broken bones of mice or moles that had fallen down the hole in years past. The sludge collected in a small puddle around the hole, then spilled over. Tumbling downhill through the bracken and bramble, it gathered momentum and volume as it found its way along a route it had not travelled for many years, forming pools behind blockages of stone or wood before either slipping through or washing them away.

The stream fell over the edge of a small hollow, into a stone basin that seemed almost hand-carved. Quickly, the water filled the Pool to the brim but did not spill over, draining instead through a hole cut into its side near the top. The mud and bones sank, coming to rest at the bottom of the basin.

In the dusk, sitting at the edge of the Dreaming Pool, the Lifeguard watched the water, now filtered and clear, glittering as if diamonds swam in its depths. She smiled to herself as the Pool began to fill.

That night, in a house on the council estate, Ben and Josh Hollward, twin boys aged nine, dreamt of a Pool in the woods, the water shining in the sunlight and of a lady standing over it, smiling at them, beckoning.

THE END

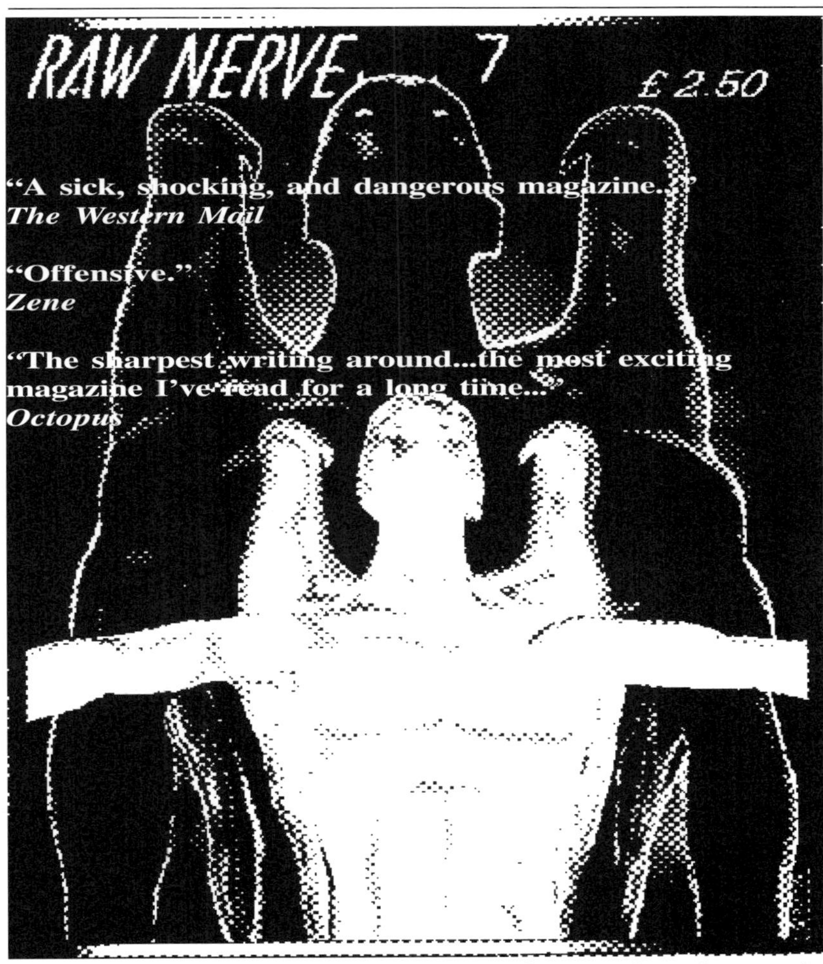
RAW NERVE 7
£2.50
"A sick, shocking, and dangerous magazine..."
The Western Mail
"Offensive."
Zene
"The sharpest writing around...the most exciting magazine I've read for a long time..."
Octopus